DELPHI AND THE GREEK WARRIOR

Other books by Lauren O. Thyme

Thymely Tales: Transformational Fairy Tales for Adults and Children,
2nd edition

Alternatives for Everyone: A Guide to Non-Traditional Health Care,
2nd edition—non-fiction

The Lemurian Way: Remembering your Essential Nature, 2nd edition

Forgiveness equals Fortune (co-authored with Liah Holtzman),
2nd edition—non-fiction

Along the Nile, a novel set in pre-dynastic Egypt, 2nd edition

From the Depths of Thyme

Strangers in Paradise, a novel of forgiveness

Cosmic Grandma Wisdom – non-fiction

Twin Souls, A Karmic Love Story

Traveling on the River of Time, a handbook for exploring past lives—
non-fiction

Catherine, Karma, and Complex PTSD— non-fiction

DELPHI AND THE GREEK WARRIOR
A novel

Lauren O. Thyme

Lauren O. Thyme Publishing
Santa Fe, New Mexico
2019

Delphi and the Greek Warrior © 2019 by Lauren O. Thyme
Lauren O. Thyme Publishing, Santa Fe, New Mexico

ISBN: 978-09983446-6-9

For information contact:
Thyme.lauren@gmail.com

LaurenOThymeCreations.com
thyme.lauren@gmail.com

Jacket/cover design:
Free images from Pixabay:
Front cover: delphi-1178710_960_720.jpg by DebraJean
Back cover: greece-300-statue-sculpture-travel-1414069 by gancheva

Special thanks to Sue Stein for her invaluable help
in editing and crafting *Delphi and the Greek Warrior.*

I dedicate this book to Donna Sandoval -
my precious friend and Selene's grandmother

Table of Contents

Chapter 1

SELENE, THE GREEK WARRIOR, AND DELPHI

Everything changes.

Saplings become trees, their leaves wrinkle and fall, only to leaf out again in the spring. Birds fledge when they're young, fly away to warmer climes, then return to make their yearly nests. Old nanny goats no longer provide milk and pass away, their bones making thick soup. Wood burns relentlessly, fire into ash. Rocks wear down from rain running over them during countless days and nights. Granite's surfaces crack during earthquakes. Even the gods seem to become weary with humans and turn their sublime faces away.

From my studies I cite the Greek poet Simonides who wrote of the fragility of life:

> *"One thousand years, ten thousand years*
> *are but a tiny dot,*
> *the smallest segment of a point,*
> *an invisible hair."*

* * *

When I was 14, I met him. My love. My darling Heraclius. I first saw him on the rocky path to Delphi. He glowed with good health and strength. As he walked up to where I stood transfixed, I thought I was in the presence of a god. Then he spoke and I was in awe of his deep, booming voice. Surely this was Zeus speaking.

I still envision Heraclius as the stalwart young man I had met all those years ago. Handsome. Brave. Athletic strength and potency like the rocks of Delphi.

Before he left for battle, his Athenian armor flashed in the sunlight as he moved. Bronze breastplate hugging his pectoral muscles, flesh and bronze cleaving to each other, as if made of the same material. Swollen bumps like nipples patterned on the metal. When he detached the straps holding the armor to his body, his warrior muscles underneath were golden-brown.

Oh, how I adored touching his bare chest, running my small fingers over his firm masculine flesh.

My hands are not as soft and supple as when I knew him. Time, grief, and travel have altered and weathered them.

* * *

I hear footsteps on the pebbled path leading to my cave. A man and woman are trudging up the precipitous terrain of Delphi to find me. To consult with me. I'm not a Delphic Oracle as my mother Xanthippe and grandmother Demetria were. No. I am simply a woman. A woman with an unrelenting gift from Apollo. A trait passed down through my lineage. My inner vision and messages from the god are more sharply in focus with every day that passes, while I huddle in my cool cavern of rock, staying out of the harsh, hot sun.

The couple spot me standing near the entrance, while I am partly hidden in shadow.

"Hello!" the man shouts. He raises his hand in greeting, squinting to make sure he has found the one he is looking for.

The woman is shy. She stands back, not able to peek at me. Grey eyes searching the ground, as if there is something to be wary of. A snake, perhaps?

Apollo's sun chariot is high in the dazzling blue sky. No clouds to block it. Intense heat sears the rocky, familiar landscape all around me. I know every turn of the path. Every rock outcropping. Each monument. I have lived here at Delphi most of my life.

"I am Selene," I declare to them.

The couple pause at the entrance. The man speaks. "We have traveled a long way to see you, Lady." He clears his throat. He reverently places some cut logs on the ground. The woman hands him two woven bags.

"Eggs. Some onions. An eggplant. Zucchini." He quickly examines one sack to verify the precious eggs are intact. Satisfied, he exhales in relief and passes them over to me.

"Thank you," I reply, my voice raspy with fatigue. I turn and set the containers against the rocky inner wall.

"And pita bread, too," the woman pipes up. "We bought some from the village below." She's not much more than a girl, a child near the age I was when I met my love. She forces a smile, although she is young and frightened, scared of facing a woman who communes with a god.

"Come," I say, motioning. "Please, step inside and sit. Get out of the heat. Be at ease." I point to a rocky platform, on which I have placed a faded pad made of strips, stuffed with wool from the spring shearing, and dried bay leaves.

Trying not to stare at me, the couple walk to the hard stone couch and seat themselves.

I place myself at their feet on the ground in front of them, reclining on an old woven carpet, a gift from my grandmother.

The three of us sit silently for a few minutes, avoiding eye contact, unsure how to begin.

I break the awkward silence. "I have some fresh goat yogurt mixed with honey from the sacred beehives here. One of the villagers brought it to me this morning. Would you like some?"

"Yes, please," the girl nods politely. She looks at the man questioningly.

He nods. On closer examination he appears to be much older than her.

I get up and scoop some of the heavenly concoction from the crock into a plain wooden bowl and hand it to the girl, along with a well-worn but clean wooden spoon.

She takes them from me gingerly, hesitantly. The young woman measures a small quantity of the thick whiteness while golden honey gathers at the edges, and holds it to the man's now-open mouth. He envelops the spoon with his lips and sucks in the delicacy. "Mmmmm," he murmurs, and licks off the remainder, grinning openly with pleasure.

"It is considered food of the gods," I mention quietly, satisfied at his enjoyment. "You, too," I encourage the young woman.

She takes the spoon from him and daintily ladles a small amount for herself and tastes it. She says nothing but her sparkling, clear grey eyes speak of delight beyond words.

When they have finished every mouthful, I take the bowl and spoon from them and place them near me in a large terracotta container of water, suitable for washing. I sit on the rug again.

Now that they are relaxed, I speak. "There is something you came here to ask me," I embolden them.

The girl blushes and looks at her feet, then up at the man.

He nods, then speaks directly to the point. "We want to marry but our families forbid it." His jaw tightens.

"Why?" I interrogate gently.

"We are from two adjoining villages who have old feuds. It is said that someone from my village stole some chickens from hers." He shrugs his shoulders. "That was long ago but still there is bad blood."

I look at the girl. "You are already pregnant."

"Yes." Her disgrace speaks through her body language and averted head.

"What shall we do?" her lover inquires earnestly, hoping for a fortunate message from Apollo.

I close my eyes. I can feel the warmth from the sun god moving from high above me to my heart area. "Apollo blesses you both," I announce after a time. "He advises you to move to yet a third village, but not too far away so that your families can visit you. In time the anger will turn to peace and eventually love."

They each nod in acknowledgement.

"Give your families—and yourselves—time to heal the bad feelings. Your child, a son, will be born healthy." When I open my eyes, I see tears running down her youthful cheeks.

She turns to the man and clings tightly to him. He strokes her wet face.

I arise, pronouncing we are finished. There is nothing more for me to say. I am used to the sudden comings and goings of messages along with the pilgrims for whom they are intended.

He stands and pulls the girl gently to her feet. I am a small woman and he towers over me. "Thank you," he tells me simply.

I smile and nod. "Took good care of the two of them."

"I will." A man of few words.

They leave my rocky home, heading down the path, stepping carefully, as not to slip on the loose gravel. The girl leans against her lover, exhausted by their long trip, the steep path, and relief. They never look back at me, as they head down the steep trail, but I am used to that, too.

For centuries the Temple of Apollo at Delphi has been paid handsomely. To reward the Temple was to ensure good luck. Statues and massive temples were built on the site. A *stadion* for athletic tournaments. A theatre. 96 marble statues along the Sacred Way. Treasuries containing substantial amounts of gold, silver, and electrum. Beautifully carved friezes of *hoplites* in battle. Beaten gold plates and bronze plaques.

Throughout the land wealthy men, armies, cities, and politicians longed to have a reading with the Delphic Sibyl regarding wartime and peacetime enterprises; political and civil controversies; intellectual, religious, and personal pursuits. They paid handsomely for the privilege and hoped for favorable results. The glory of the Delphic Oracle had grown steadily for hundreds of years while the Temple became rich beyond imaging.

But I am not an Oracle. Have never been an Oracle.

Yet I know I have done well this day and the god is happy with me, the most important payment I can receive. That and being grateful I had positive news to tell the couple, which isn't always the case. My job is to speak honestly and simply so there is no doubt of the message. Truth is always better than a lie, no matter how well intentioned. I have clarity that an Oracle may be lacking, perhaps from the vapors overwhelming her mind while seated on the tripod within the inner shrine of Apollo, the hallowed *Adyton.*

The sweetness of today's message resonates through me, as though my smile can be felt from tip to toe. I look around my cave. A secluded home, austere and simple. Remembering the period I spent traveling with Kriton and the other soldiers, sleeping outside in the elements, in good weather and bad. Looking for Heraclius. I would have never suspected when I was a girl, deeply in love, that I would live alone in my elongated stone abode near the top of holy Mt. Parnassus.

I believe I am performing sacred service and thus my life has meaning. Many people come to consult with me. They bring me payment in the form of presents. Food. Olive oil. Honey. Firewood to keep me warm at night. Blankets to keep me warm. A *chiton* to clothe me. Whatever pilgrims think I need and they can afford.

I straighten my unadorned *peplos* that comes to just below my knees. My legs are skinny although at one time when I was younger I was shapely and attractive, so Demetria, my grandmother told me. She was a dear soul, a loving woman, unlike my mother Xanthippe who was argumentative and unsympathetic.

The three of us lived near the village below Delphi, not far from the Temple complex, in a white-washed stucco house built for us. Rules had been loosened to allow the three of us to live in the same abode. No men were allowed in the family sanctorum, although both my mother and grandmother had secret lovers and each became pregnant once. My grandmother Demetria bore my mother. My mother Xanthippe gave birth to me, Selene, a name that refers to the moon, perhaps from her moonlit trysts.

They were both good-looking women, not to mention they were known as Pythias or Sibyls, Oracles of Apollo. They were considered superior, and revered by all. However, we were not allowed to marry nor have families, according to the tenets of Delphi.

My mother and her mother bickered constantly. How to cut an onion properly. How to debone a chicken. How to sweep the matted floor so the dust didn't rise up and make one of them sneeze. What the proper way was to go about receiving messages from Apollo. On and on, day after day. One might have thought that they would eventually tire of the game.

Demetria, Xanthippe and I possessed the second sight. The ability ran through us, so there was never a question we would become Oracles when we were old enough. However, I decided for myself at 9 years old, that the life and role of Priestess was not suitable for me. I wanted a normal life, including a husband and children, and to live outside of the holy strictures. The prestige of being a Sibyl didn't appeal to me. I desired to be free and unencumbered by the onerous responsibilities of having visions and messages come through me from Apollo, those messages often deciding the fate of powerful men, politicians, armies, even city-states.

The moment when my mother Xanthippe found out about my plan to decline the honor of becoming a Sibyl, Hades itself trembled.

She took hold of me by the chin so I had to look up at her. "What do you mean?! A normal life? Ha! We are special. Don't you understand that? You want to throw all of it away and try to survive like the village women around here, as nothing. To be mere property of a man. You ungrateful girl! After all I have done for you. Without me you would be nobody. You'd be plucking chickens, milking goats, and having a dozen snot faced children running after you, whining and complaining. Along with an ungrateful, arrogant husband. Is that what you want?"

"Leave the child alone," Grandmother gently interrupted Xanthippe in her lengthy harangue. Saving me from her fury once again.

"You stay out of this, old woman," Xanthippe snarled. "You're always spoiling her."

"Now, daughter…" but she wasn't allowed to finish.

"We will talk about this later. Meanwhile she is under MY control."

"All right. All right," Demetria temporized, trying to placate her daughter Xanthippe. "Yes, let us not argue about this anymore."

My mother folded her arms over her ample chest, breasts slightly sagging, aging belly protuberant, smirking, as if she had won the battle. She didn't understand the power of water dripping on a stone, eventually changing its shape and size.

A raven cawed, perched on an olive tree outside, the sound emphasizing the moment of Xanthippe's triumph inside our home.

No one knew that, unlike her charming demeanor at work as an Oracle, my mother could be a harridan, especially when crossed. None of her lovers knew that aspect of Xanthippe unless they spent a great deal of time with her, which didn't usually happen. Her time outside the home was limited and she was carefully guarded and protected, although she and Demetria had ways of eluding observation when they intended.

While having a lover was officially frowned upon, for generations Sibyls had used the potent herb *silphium* to prevent pregnancy. *Silphium* was the essential item of trade from the city of Cyrene, and was so critical to the Cyrenian economy that most of their coins bore a picture of the plant. *Silphium* was used widely by most of the Mediterranean cultures, considering it worth its weight in silver coins.

Legend said that the herb was a gift from the god Apollo, which made it even more appropriate for Oracles to partake of it. Another plant, asafoetida, could be used as a cheaper substitute for *silphium*, and had similar enough qualities. But the Oracles dared not use the alternative, for fear of pregnancy, being cast out of society, or even stoned to death. Marriage was not an option.

* * *

The couple picks their way down the steep slope, making sure not to slide on the stones, keeping their footfalls short and sure. He has his arm around her waist, thickening with life. Do they love each other? Will their love last? Those answers didn't come to me during our time in the cave. All I heard is their families will relent and make peace for the sake of the child. That is the ecstatic function of being a visionary, bringing valuable news, even for an unofficial oracle as I am today.

The lengthening shadows haunt my simple home. The stone is getting cold and damp with night. Although the mountain is sweltering by day, once the sun begins to set at this altitude, evening chills the rocky expanse.

I speak to the shadows. "Are my mother and grandmother proud of me from their perspective in the underworld? Do they forgive me for breaking the noble family tradition of the Delphic Oracle? Can you tell me who my father is, the unknown figure from my mother's past?"

My birthright is a hushed secret, not revealed to anyone, nor spoken of even in whispers because of the sacred tradition of Delphic celibacy.

The shadows say nothing, remaining mute to my thoughts and queries.

Evening approaches. Wind whistles through my cave, mocking me with inscrutable messages. I wrap a long *himation* around my shoulders to warm myself until I can get a fire going with the wood given to me today as a sacred offering.

Earlier in my life I tried to argue with the Fates. I chose a lover instead of becoming the next Delphic Oracle. The man left to fight glorious battles. I gave birth to his boy-child. A man from the great city-state of Athens married me and adopted the son. Nonetheless I abandoned my husband and the youngster to find my lover. Though the outcome is now clear, I would still walk the same path towards my difficult future.

Perhaps I intuited the conclusion even at the beginning of our affair, but love is a stubborn wound that often refuses to heal, even with the best of intentions. Neutrality, lack of feeling, is the only solution. I wasn't able to create that calm inside me. It is a mystery that I could love the faithless, perplexing man. And still do.

Maybe I wasn't strong enough with the spirit of Apollo inside me to be an Oracle. Possibly I was connected to Aphrodite instead, with her overwhelming, sensuous urges and whimsical lovers, unfaithful with many men to her crippled husband Hephaistos and their marriage bed. Is that why I was drawn to Heraclius? Who became a warrior in the same fashion as Ares, Aphrodite's most famous paramour? Although I've been Seer for many, I cannot see myself.

"Tell me, I beg you, Apollo. Reveal what I need to know," I beseech him.

The god remains silent.

As an Oracle-in-training I was well-educated. I recall a passage from Euripides' play Hippolytus that echoes my own turmoil:

> *"Eros, Eros, melting desire in the eyes*
> *sweet delight in the souls*
> *of all your victims,*
> *come to me never,*
> *never if not in peace;*
> *never upset my mind,*
> *dance with me out of time…"*

Chapter 2

THE CAVE AGE 12 438 BC

From my viewpoint standing on the patch of dirt in front of our little white house I can see the children of Delphi village playing. Our cottage isn't part of the community, but is situated on the outskirts, far from residents and pilgrims alike.

Children are not allowed to be near me. They are considered unclean, while my mother, grandmother, and I are pure. My home and my family are sacrosanct thus I cannot associate with the masses. Thus I am alone in my holiness.

I don't want to be holy. I want to play with other children. Screech and run through the hills and get dirty, be a part of the community, and forgo loneliness. Yearning to be a part of their carefree lives, I sometimes cry myself to sleep in my solitude.

Watching the youngsters from this distance, my sadness arises. My teeth clenched tightly together, I command the friendless pain in my gut to leave me. Hum a tuneless song, kick a pebble at my feet, and pretend I am fine. The stone buildings and the glory of this place do not impress me. I would rather be part of village life, instead of cast away into the complicated domains of Oracles, Priests, treasuries and cold marble statues. Statues don't soothe me. They are unresponsive to my desire for comfort and affection.

Why did the Fates decree I would be born into my family? This place? This life? I want to be a conventional girl living an ordinary existence. Would I know how to manage living as a mundane person? No, but I would like to try and am willing to learn. To achieve a normalcy that the village women do not comprehend as uninteresting. Husbands, laundry, cooking, gardening, and children are the epicenter of their lives. Could I be part of their communal existence, humdrum though it might be?

My grandmother finds me outside. "Oh, there you are, Selene. I have been looking for you. Did you have something to eat?"

"Yes, grandmama. I had some pita bread dipped in olive oil, yogurt, and some dried dates."

"That is good," she replies kindly. "Olives have been properly brined and are ready to eat. Would you like some of those? You need to put more meat on your bones, dear one. You are too skinny as it is."

I smile at her. Demetria means well and is not scolding me as Xanthippe does. "I love you, Grandma," I tell her.

"I love you too, Selene." She enters our house.

Our home is more comfortable than any peasant's hut in Delphi village. It contains three bedrooms, one in front for grandmother, and another for me at the far end, with a large chamber for my mother in the middle. An *oikos* for company is located to the right of the front door; while a *gyneceum* is situated to the left, a chamber for girls, women, and small children only. A kitchen is set off in one area, next to the *gyneceum*, with a simple wood table and stools and a separate storage area, with a door to the outside courtyard where the round earthenware oven is located. There is a small patio with a tiled roof to shade the intense sunlight. Greek houses often contain an *andron* as well, which is exclusively for men, but no men live in this house.

The throngs of pilgrims are absent in Delphi at this time. Today includes one of the three passes of the moon when the Oracle is not in residence at the Temple of Apollo. Where my mother Xanthippe is honored as Pythia, the Oracle. My grandmother is also a Pythia, has been in residence before her daughter Xanthippe came of age, and sometimes still performs the oracular task when needed. Visitors congregate in the *Adyton*, a cleft in the mountain that houses the sacred grotto, where the Pythia, my mother, sits on Apollo's tripod throne swooning in ecstasy. She listens to the god's words, revealing messages to eager travelers.

But today no masses of men are clamoring for answers. No government officials are present, looking influential, waving vital documents in the face of the Priest. No one is frantically bathing in the icy Castalian Spring, praying to be first in line. No priests scurrying here and there collecting massive fees and donations. No sacrifices of goats to appease the god.

Simple tranquility this day; a dry, predictable day. A few clouds gather at the top of Mt. Parnassus as the mountain creates its own weather. All around me flowers are blossoming in the spring sunshine, flourishing in cracks and crevices of the slope where water has been deposited from rainfall and winter snow. Crocus are dying out, while daffodils are bursting into bloom, their yellow heads nodding gracefully in the wind. During the heat of summer wild grasses will grow tall, when orange and yellow calendulas proliferate.

Glancing up the steep hill above Delphi that I have never been bold enough to climb, I make a momentous decision. Today I will ascend the dusty, stony trail that leads ever higher towards Mt. Parnassus. Past marble buildings, temples and treasuries. Between the pair of cliffs called Phaedriades above the Castalian Spring, where Oracles, Priests and pilgrims cleanse themselves in the holy water.

In ancient times Zeus released two sacred eagles from opposite ends of the earth to find the center. The eagles met at Delphi. Then Apollo slew Python, a demonic serpent, near the Castalian spring that bubbles up near the cleft in the mountain where the Oracle, my mother sits, listening to the prophecies of the god in the *Adyton*. The naval stone, a marble Omphales, is placed at the entrance to the *Adyton*, while small carvings of the omphalos are given as votive offerings to pilgrims.

Several times I had ventured partway up the incline, but always got called back home, where I was forced to sit inside my gloomy and unpleasant home. There, two unhappy women berated each other while I pretended to be invisible.

I run along flagged pathways, near temporarily-closed buildings, treasuries, and Temples, to the unpaved trail to Mt. Parnassus, and start hiking. The path is a steep climb and my breathing grows labored. Below me I see the valley of Phocis, a vast and overwhelming chasm at the bottom of the mountain. I am alone on the footpath. Village children are not allowed on this track.

Girls of the community, regardless of age, are all children. They are unaware of the mysteries of men, men's demands, and the wars men incite on each other. These girls will remain childlike until old age. Then they will cross the river Styx, ignorant of anything more significant than village life, cleaning, cooking, and eventually and periodically having babies.

If a woman gives birth to a boy child, she is praised, as boys grow up to be men and have value, while girls and women do not. Therefore girl children are not celebrated. They are less than a bug at one's feet. Girls are merely possessions like a goat or a water bladder or at best a tiny plot of land. Boys are taught mysteries, histories of gods and heroes that are not privy to girls. When boys grow up they become warriors, fight momentous battles, and become celebrated heroes like Odysseus.

However, the men of Delphi village will not become heroes. They haul heavy rocks, stones, and marble to build monuments, their faces sweaty, their muscles straining, calling out to each other in their working partnerships. They till the unyielding soil near their homes in order to create gardens and grow food. Create shelters for goats and chickens. No Delphi man has ever become a warrior nor ventured off to battle. They are needed here to care for the colossal sacred precinct called the Temple of Delphi—and their own families.

However, I'm neither a woman nor a man, but a young ignorant girl, isolated from village knowledge. Bleeding has not yet commenced for me. Both women of my home have instructed me on this mystery. The experience in which I must unwillingly participate seems dreadful to me.

"You will be a woman, then," my mother nods meaningfully.

"I don't care. I don't want to bleed," I tell her. I have memories of villagers who have been hurt and bled profusely. Several of them died of their wounds. I had no need to be a woman, especially if I would die of bleeding.

The woman's curse apparently comes every month. Every month I could bleed to death. A game of chance to tempt death every 28 days Could that be why women are worthless, because they can die any month?

The only woman of value in the whole of the Greek world is the Delphic Oracle, treated with utmost respect and deference by everyone. She is tended to, cared for, and educated. The Oracle is paradoxically always a woman, a prophetic woman, in spite of the lowly status that women generally hold.

Men voyage from all over the known world to seek an audience, to have an opportunity for a holy message from Apollo through the female Pythia, while women are excluded from attending. Kings need to appreciate and ascertain their empires. Politicians want to attest to the status and wellbeing of their cities and citizens. Generals must confirm the outcome of battles and wars.

My mother once told me a tale of Croesus who had sought a reading at Delphi. "He was richer than any king alive. He received a message from the Oracle, but the Priest misunderstood the words, and because of that, Croesus lost his kingdom." She chuckled cynically, shaking her head at the absurdity of men.

The oracular Sibyl has been an institution for hundreds of years. People couldn't remember when an Oracle was non-existent.

Except for the Oracles, girls and women are not taught any knowledge whatsoever. They have no need of learning, although their jobs are just as hard as men, and as backbreaking. Tending the crops, milking the goats, harvesting honey, doing laundry, cleaning their homes, cooking meals, bearing and raising children. Both men and women from the village work from sun up to sundown in unrelenting toil.

However, I do not have to labor. As an Oracle-in-training I am privileged, having no work to perform except to learn and expand myself into the world of the god. Listening to Apollo and passing on his messages is of vital significance.

Because of my celebrated family, I am given papyrus to study instead of employing physical labor. I learn to read, write, and study mathematics. Along with that, I acquire the ability to understand maps so that as a Sibyl I will be able to articulate a message about faraway lands.

While I muse about these weighty issues, I stop to wipe my forehead, which is dripping with sweat from the exertion of the climb. The path meanders upwards. Mt. Parnassus rises high above me, snow still showing near the peak, not having yet fully melted in the spring thaw.

Then I see it. The cave. Like a welcoming womb in the cleft of the rocks. Taller than the tallest man. Three times as wide as it is tall. Coolness exudes from the opening. Although not evident from the outside, the cave reaches into the mountain formation the height of two people laying head to toe. Ashes from old bonfires, perhaps ancient, are evident; the ceiling and the stony floor blackened from those fires. Bones from cooked animals are everywhere.

The cavern beckons like an old friend. I obey. The floor inside is flat. Towards the middle is a level stone, almost the size of my bed but higher. I walk over and clamber on top. The cold from the stone is chilling to my backside, so I slide off.

Sensations of peace along with a feeling of being at home radiate that I have never experienced anywhere else in Delphi. anywhere in Delphi. Certainly not in my family home. I have an irresistible urge to clean the grotto and make it spotless as a shrine.

I scramble down the path, back to our house. My grandmother is sitting at a loom in the *gyneceum*, the woman's room, where she is weaving cloth that will be dyed yellow and fashioned into chitons. Later she will collect shearing from the local sheep to weave into warm himations.

Xanthippe, my mother, is not in residence. I wonder about her absence since it isn't the time of the Pythia. Could she have gone to the village? Unlikely, though, since crones from the hamlet bring us everything we need.

I nod at Demetria but the grand dame is dozing at her weaving and doesn't see me. I grab old cloths from a basket where we keep them. I dip them in a crock of water near the door, quietly wring them out, seize our well-used broom, and struggle back up to the grotto.

I am panting and out of breath by the time I again reach the cave. This is my new home. I grin. No one will disturb me or tell me what to do here. It is utterly tranquil.

Once I recover from the climb, I wipe down the couch-like stone, then sweep out ashes, charred pieces of wood, and animal bones from the floor of my new secret location. What to do with debris? There is a natural gully outside following the path down to the valley. When it rains, it should wash the wreckage away. I brush the rubbish into the gully.

My work has occupied me for a long time and I fail to notice the sun is setting. I leave the rags in the cave, but take the broom home with me. It will be missed. All the way back I beam, arriving before dark, and return the broom to its customary place.

"Where have you been Selene?" Xanthippe complains as I rush in.

"Just exploring," I tell her truthfully.

"Be careful. You could get hurt." She is standing at the inside table, busy stuffing a *kotopoulo*, a chicken, with figs, mint leaves, lemon slices, and brined olives for our dinner. She dumps it into a *tapsi*, a traditional clay pan, and takes it to bake in the outside oven. Dinner is served late, after the heat of the day passes. Usually two village women, Portia and Kleida, care for us. They must be busy today as Xanthippe is doing the cooking herself.

"Yes, mother, I will take care," I call after her. I can hardly wait until the sun is up the next day so I can return to my cave. I hope I sleep well tonight.

Demetria is at her loom weaving, awake now. I walk over and give her a hug.

"What are you so happy about, child?"

"Oh, nothing," I retort, smirking to myself about my clandestine plans. "Did you have a good nap?"

"It's my age. I seem to fall asleep easily without even knowing it. Especially in the afternoon."

"Old woman! Come out here and help me!" Xanthippe shouts. "I'm trying to bake some pita bread."

"Yes, yes. I'm on my way." My grandmama gets up unsteadily from her seat and limps outside, somewhat bent over, with a dowagers hump beginning to be noticeable. She is aging quickly nowadays. What would life be like without her? Perhaps finding the cave today is divine timing from Apollo. The cave will also make a good hiding place from my mother.

* * *

Next morning I eat a little leftover chicken, some yogurt, brined olives, and a hunk of day-old chewy pita bread to dunk in the yogurt. I am ready to leave the house to head up the path. The day is sunny while the path continues to be clear and dry. The sun gleams off our white stucco house. The monuments of the Temple dazzle the eye.

"Where are you going?" my mother inquires, still drowsy in the early morning light.

"I'll be home by lunch time," I respond, a non-answer to avoid unpleasant questions that could lead to losing my new play space.

I practically run up the steep hill, stopping now and then to take a deep breath, hold my aching side, and then continue.

When I arrive I exclaim, "I forgot the broom!" I don't want to return until I recover from the climb. I gather blackened bones from the cooking pit, deposit them in a rag, then pull the cloth outside to the gully, and dump the remains. I repeat this action time after time until I have transferred a huge heap of bones to the culvert outdoors. I address the pile out loud, a habit from being alone so often. "I hope I'm right, that a rainstorm will wash you down the hill." I grimace, contemplating problems that could occur, both with and without rain.

My hands are filthy from the bones and wood ash. I have no water so I move outside and rub my hands on the stony dust. Then I finish the job, first waving the soiled cloth in the wind then wiping my hands on the grimy rag. I sit on the couch-stone, sweaty and dirty, too tired to care if I get my *chiton* dirty, while I ignore the coldness to my skinny behind.

Then I remember my mother Xanthippe who will scold me if I am late. Sighing in concern and fatigue, I wonder. What makes her irritable? She's almost never happy. Xanthippe is a puzzle I have never been able to figure out. Perhaps she will be cheerier with me gone from the house. I vow to climb the hill to my new cave as often as possible.

As I sit on the couch-stone, a parade of ants streams across the enclosure towards the entrance. Engrossed with them, I don't notice that the sun has climbed to its zenith. Time for lunch.

I grab the dirty cloths and hurry down the hill. Halfway down in my rush I slip on some gravel and fall to the ground, scraping my right knee. "Oh, ye gods, Xanthippe will surely be angry with me now!" I exclaim, limping on, favoring my leg, while being more careful about my footing.

The path towards my family house seems longer than before. As I zig and zag around the massive shrines along the Sacred Way, the house finally materializes.

Xanthippe is standing at the doorway, her hands on her generous hips, scowling. "Where have you been for so long? What have you been doing? You're a dirty mess. Look at your knee!"

I hang my head. "I'm sorry, mama. I was playing and fell down."

"Tsk, tsk," she retorts. "Come over to the water jar and let me wash you off."

"I can do it myself. I'm a big girl," but she grabs my wrist and pulls me over, proceeding to remove my clothing, and soaking me with water. "Demetria," she cries out. "Bring me a clean *chiton* for Selene and a cloth to dry her off. Some honey too, for her wound."

My grandmother isn't immediately forthcoming, so Xanthippe hollers loudly. "Mother!!!"

"Yes, I'm on my way." The older woman slowly appears with some cloths and my *chiton*.

"Honey, too. Don't forget the honey."

"Here it is." Demetria hands over the small clay container with the precious honey to my mother.

Once I am cleaned, dried, and clothed, Xanthippe has me sit on a one of our 3-legged wooden stools outside under the roof. "Let's see it." She examines my wound. "Not too bad. You must be more careful, Selene." She applies a small amount of honey to my scraped knee.

"Ow!" I wriggle in protest, the wound tender to her touch.

"Hold still. I'm almost done." She wipes her honeyed finger on the used rag. "There. Now sit in the sun and let it dry." Xanthippe has forgotten her interrogation of my whereabouts and how I came to injure myself.

"Yes, mother, I will."

She wipes her forehead with the back of her hand, then gathers the dirty items and heads inside. I can hear her talking to grandmamma. "We will need to get these and the other laundry items to Portia. She hasn't been here in a while."

"Portia should be here soon."

Xanthippe interrupts her. "I hope Portia comes today. We need clean clothes."

Chapter 3

APOLLO   AGE 13   437 BC

Every day except during rainy or snowy weather or when studying scrolls for my education, I climb to the cave. I clean the space thoroughly and often, so that no traces from the past can be detected. Once while standing on the couch-stone, I reach high above me in order to clean the blackened ceiling above it. Using stale urine added to water in a container, the mixture is strong enough to remove layers of soot from cooking fires. There are places I can't reach, so I resign myself to an almost-spotless space.

Laboriously I sweep the ground of wood ash and remaining bones, wash layers of dirt, dust, and grime from the stony walls and the couch-stone until they gleam.

It takes me more days to cut and sew an elongated thick cushion in the length and width of the couch-stone made from cloth, stitched on three sides. Then I fill it with tufts of wool from Delphi's yearly sheep shearing, dried bay leaves, and remnants of fabric. Next I sew the remaining edge closed. This I do by hand, using needle and thread from Demetria's ample stockpile of sewing items, along with old and discarded leather strips, fabric and worn clothing, which I fashion for the cover. I use the heftiest pieces I can find for the casing, since the jagged rocky surface from the couch-stone will wear out the shell quickly. The cushion is lumpy, but thickly comfortable, while the chill from the stone is eliminated. My fingertips are sore from numerous pinpricks but my mission is complete.

Pleased with my work, I sit on the couch-stone cushion and examine my exertions with pleasure. The cave project surprisingly gladdens my heart. I have an aptitude as well as enjoyment for simple physical tasks.

Then I conceive of a far-reaching plan, to make full use of both study and solitude. I will surreptitiously bring scrolls to my cave, to merge my education with newfound personal independence. Studying while in my grotto deepens the breadth, depth, and comprehension of what I read. Never again will I be lonely or bored.

One morning, weeks after my plan has commenced, I wake up with strange pain low in my belly. When I arise from my mattress, I notice blood.

I cry out. "Grandmama!"

Demetria rushes in and sees where I am pointing. "Ah, yes. Now you are a woman. This bleeding is normal for a girl, as we have explained to you for some time."

"Oh." I am filled with disappointment and desolation. "What good is it for?" I question. "To bleed and have pain?"

"So you are able to have babies," she continues then realizes her error.

"Oracles don't have babies," I argue. My brows furrow. "Except you and mama."

"It is complicated, Selene," Demetria starts to explain, then changes the subject. "Your breasts will grow…"

"Large like Xanthippe?" I interrupt.

"I don't know. We shall see. Mine are small." She points to my various body parts. "Hair will grow down there and under here. Perhaps it already does."

"Becoming a woman is a peculiar adaptation to undergo," I snivel wretchedly. "I don't want to do this. Can I avoid it?"

"No, dearest one. All women go through this when they reach a certain age, while the bleeding occurs every 28 days or so. It is called menarche."

"Do you bleed?"

"I have achieved what is known as menopause. My bleeding times don't come any more." She takes my hand and we go to the rag bin together. "You will need to use cloths to absorb the blood." She hands a thick one to me. "Here also is a strip of leather to tie around your waist to hold the cloth in place." She shows me how to secure it.

I reluctantly strap on the cloth. "This isn't fair. What do boys have to go through?"

"They have to study and learn."

"I learn and study."

"Yes, that is true. Men make a vocation for themselves in life. Sometimes they fight wars."

"I'll do it! I'll make a vocation. I'll go fight wars! If only I don't have to..."

Demetria shakes her head in compassion. "The gods have made us women as we are. There is no use in trying to change what cannot be altered. You will only make yourself miserable."

"Is that why mother is unhappy, because she cannot change herself? Is bleeding why women have no value?"

"Selene. Let us not talk of this anymore." My ever-patient grandmother has become exasperated.

"All right," I agree reluctantly like the balky donkey from the village. "I apologize."

"Selene, I am sorry I cannot make things different for you." Then she hugs me. When I look at her, I see a few stray tears running down her aging, wrinkling cheeks. I feel regret for hurting her feelings.

Although I grumble and complain, I finally accept that I have become a woman, in all its manifestations and complications.

I continue to take scrolls to study in my cave.

On the day Xanthippe discovers I am sneaking scrolls out of the house, she is upset at first, but quickly acquiesces. "You must promise me that you will care for every scroll as if it is a newborn lamb. Scrolls are precious, loaned to us from wealthy and powerful men who travel long distances to reach Delphi. Guard the parchments like gold. These documents take a long time to be written, and often cannot be replaced," she concludes her lecture.

"I will, Mother," I promise. "I had no idea of their value."

"Well, now you do."

"Mother," I hesitate, bashful, but curious. "Do you bleed? Grow hair in odd places?"

"Yes. Why do you ask?"

"Because I started bleeding several days ago."

"Makes sense," states Xanthippe. "That is also when I started bleeding."

"Isn't that a strange coincidence?" I murmur.

"No, not at all," my mother explains. "When women live together, their menstrual cycles synchronize."

"Why?"

"You will travel into the underworld with the word why on your lips!" Xanthippe brusquely leaves my side and our conversation is at an end.

Some weeks after my discussion with Xanthippe, I am seated on the couch-stone in my cave, reading a play about the Persian Wars by Aeschylus. His words are disturbing. Women in his play are portrayed as evil, cunning or feather-headed, certainly not to be trusted. Only men are trustworthy. I lay the papyrus cylinder aside to consider.

"Apollo," I summon the god. He sometimes comes to me when I call and we have exchanges. He has become my best, my only, friend. I can hear his words and feel meanings. Seldom do I have visions, but the other two techniques are adequate for communication. "What do you think of the play I'm reading?" I ask him.

"How does it make you feel?" the god questions, like an invisible questioning Socrates.

"I feel... sad. Confused. Are women evil and cunning?"

"What do you think?"

"It seems to depend on an individual person. People are unique, each one different."

"That is a suitable answer," the god responds.

"Why does Aeschylus judge women harshly?"

"That is a good question, Selene."

"Thank you. Do you have an answer for me?"

"An answer may only strengthen Aeschylus' opinion of good versus bad."

"I see. Is there no such thing as good and bad?"

"What do you think?"

"From what little I experience, every person has some of each quality inside. Neither all good nor all bad."

"Well done, Selene. Very philosophical," the god compliments me. "You are growing with knowledge and wisdom."

"What is wisdom?" I probe.

"Wisdom is loftier than knowledge. With knowledge, one can apprehend certain details. History. Philosophy. Mathematics. Understanding a map. Reading a play or poetry. Whereas wisdom occurs with time, experience, and age. Yet not all people are able to attain wisdom."

"Hmmm," I comment. "Why is that?"

"Because," the god pauses for emphasis, "attaining wisdom is often inherent in one's total makeup. A quality one is born with and can develop. For example, some people can play the flute. But only a certain talented individual can master the flute, making people happy or sad with their music, stirring their empathies, and communing with the

Muses. The same thing is true of wisdom. It is similar to being an Oracle, which is inborn in your family. You three are chosen by me to deliver my messages. No one else has those qualities as you do."

"Really? Why?" Since I have limited familiarity with people, I have no idea what Apollo is talking about.

"Demetria embodies the qualities of love, kindness, compassion, and patience. She is quiet, obedient, and accepting. While Xanthippe is often fiery, easily annoyed, and discontented. She is born with those attributes. She has an unquenchable longing for a bigger world than what she can inhabit. She wishes to be something other than what she is. Her desire is to be a midwife, but that occupation may be closed to her. Then there is you."

"Me?"

"You question everything. While you are training to be an Oracle, you go far beyond that ability. You learn, question, challenge, and argue. You want to know why. What is common knowledge or what is written by others is not good enough for you. You have a desire to comprehend more. To know everything. Plus you feel deeply; a virtuoso of emotion. You are mistaken if you think that all people are like you. They are not. Demetria can appreciate you, but she isn't like you. Xanthippe doesn't understand you at all and doesn't care to know."

"I appreciate this information. We three are different, although we are related by blood and live in the same house."

"The differences in a family or a village are not unusual. The ancient Babylonians had a system of studying the sky for information to explain these anomalies."

"Do you mean astronomy?"

"They termed the practice astrology. Accordingly the planets, sun and moon determine one's characteristics as well as one's fate, depending on date, time, and place of birth."

Apollo seems to be finished for the day. "It is time for you to return home. They are waiting." With that the voice becomes silent. The presence is gone.

My constant comings and goings have ceased to be a subject of controversy, so nothing is mentioned when I arrive. I descend from my cave in time for dinner that Kleida prepared and delivered.

She has fried a quantity of fresh barbouni, a small fish often eaten whole. "As you know, we are far from the Aegean Sea, so seafood is a special treat. You must eat it quickly before it spoils."

Demetria tells Kleida "Take some of the fish for yourself."

"No, thank you," the woman replies courteously. "These were brought especially for you as a present from Aegeus, an Athenian merchant who owns a fleet of ships. He consults the Oracle when he is here, which is often. He also brought a large octapodi, which he ordered beaten well to tenderize it. I will cut up the tentacles and fry them in olive oil for supper tomorrow. In addition, his gifts to Apollo include rice and many spices from the east. You will feast better than most kings. For the time being at least."

"Please help yourself to some fish. You deserve it, Kleida," my mother Xanthippe encourages. "You work hard for us, in addition to your own family and chores."

"Serving you is my honor, mistress," Kleida answers, her eyes lowered in respect. Kleida's standing in the community is superior to other village women except Portia because of their service to us, an uncommon boon to them and their families.

Inside, the house is sweltering. Thus we move our 3-legged stools outside to the patio, to the well-worn table, the wood cracking and peeling from the incessant glare of the sun, and sit. We eat the barbouni with our bare hands, licking our fingers periodically. Fish heads are an especially luscious delicacy. There isn't much meat in the head so we nibble delicately with our teeth and then suck the eyes out as well, savoring, swallowing in delight.

"Delicious!" I exclaim, reaching for more.

"You have outdone yourself once again, dear Kleida," compliments Demetria.

"Thank you, mistress. I am gratified to be of service."

Chapter 4

HERACLIUS   AGE 14   436 BC

Heading down the mountain after my daily sojourn in my cave, I have the scroll tucked carefully under my arm.

Suddenly I hear footsteps quickly approaching. Closer. Who can it be? No one ever walks this upper path but me. Sometimes I see pilgrims down on the Sacred Way but not higher up. I stop at a bend in the path. The summer sun is glaring in my eyes and I can't see. I put my hand up to my eyes, to shield them, to discern who is charging up the hill.

A tall young man has stopped on the path just below me. He's dressed only in a fustanella, a short skirt fastened at the waist by a leather strap. Chest, arms and legs are bare and he is wearing simple sandals, the straps tied around his ankles.

"Who are you?" I ask curtly. Xanthippe would be angry at me for speaking thus. I have been up and down this path so many times I have become possessive of it, and towards all the land around it as well. The cave is mine, too, of course.

"I am Heraclius." He smiles beguilingly, not the least upset. "Who are you?" he asks. "Are you a wood nymph come to steal my soul? Or to put a spell upon me?" he teases.

"I am called Selene."

"Ah, Goddess of the Moon."

My breath sticks in my chest and I gasp in recognition. This man is familiar. But from where? How could that be? I never go anywhere. Never see anyone except my mother and grandmother. Except for Portia from the village, who looks after us, and Kleida, too. But never a man. Unless one counts Apollo as a man and not a god.

Heraclius appears like a marble statue. To my scrutinizing eyes he is a flawless specimen of a man, with the perfect body formula, called the Golden Ratio, the letter phi. This mathematical quotient is used by architects, mathematicians, and artists to produce objects of great beauty, such as temples and the buildings at Delphi.

Although he has perfect Greek dimensions, he isn't a statue. He is a living man. An exquisite one at that. He stands half-naked, wearing little more than his short, pleated skirt. Bronzed hairless skin gleams, having been doused with olive oil, which is rubbed off with a strigil. I have read about this technique used by athletes. His face is scraped clean of whiskers as well

He affirms my evaluation. "I am in training for the Pythian Games and thought I would use this mountain footway to strengthen my muscles. To increase my stamina as well. Have you ever attended the Games?"

"No," I react. "I am not allowed out in public."

Wrinkling his forehead, he continues. "Why not?"

"It is not seemly for a girl. Especially not for the daughter and granddaughter of the Pythia."

"You must be lonely, then," he responds bluntly.

With those words, he reminds me of my isolation. "I am," I answer honestly. "But this is the route the god wants me to travel. To live this life. To be the next Oracle."

"Is that so?" he questions me.

"Yes," I lower my voice, "except I don't want to be an Oracle," fearing that someone will hear and report my dissatisfaction to Temple authorities.

"Is there a place we can sit?" he inquires. "In order to have a proper conversation."

"There's the...my...cave up above," I confide. "Would that be suitable?"

"Show me."

"This way." With trepidation, I turn and start back up the steep trail. Heraclius silently follows.

When we arrive at the cave, I motion him to go inside.

He sits on the couch-stone cushion, making himself comfortable, examining the cavern as he does so. His muscular calves and thighs are well-developed, while his pectoral muscles seem to be sculpted out of fleshy clay. His eyes are startlingly green, the color of moss that grows on the north side of rocks during the rainy season.

"This is your cave?" he jokes with me again.

"I found it. No one else comes here. Just me." I sit on the ground in front of him, on a faded woven rug given to Demetria years before.

"And now me, your first guest. It's quite cozy. What do you do here?"

"I study. Sometimes hear things."

"Hear what?"

I blush. I have never confided in anyone except my trusted grandmother Demetria. "Messages from Apollo. He talks with me."

"Really? Apollo himself? But not in the *Adyton* below?"

"No." I hesitate. "I have never been in the sacred place. Only my mother and Demetria, my grandmother. She says that I have the gift that runs in our family."

"The gift of what?" he probes.

"The gift from Apollo, the god of prophecy," I answer.

Although Heraclius must be close to my age, he seems much older. He exudes a manliness, a physicality that makes my head pulse. He is extremely tall, with long arms and legs. His skirt barely covers his upper legs. I am dizzy from the heat of the day—and Heraclius.

He stares at me as though I am a feral creature from the mountains. What did he call me? A wood nymph?

"I don't mean to upset you," he continues congenially. "I am delighted to find you on this trail. In this wild place. Thank you for showing me your cave."

"You're welcome," I reply, more courteous now, having composed myself after my earlier shock.

"I'm sorry to have disturbed you, Selene of the Moon."

"You haven't disturbed me, Heraclius," I reply.

He stands up, gazing down at me. "I must be going. To continue my training."

"So soon?"

"My sponsor Aegeus will be missing me."

Yes, of course," I consent. "Is that the same Aegeus that brought us wonderful food?"

"Most likely," he answers. "Aegeus is a wealthy merchant, with many ships. When he comes to consult the Pythia, he often brings items to Delphi from other lands."

"The food was superb," I continue.

"I will be in Delphi for a few weeks of training followed by the Pythia Games. May I come visit you in your cave again, perhaps tomorrow?"

"Tomorrow?? Um…I'm not supposed to be around anyone. Especially not a man."

"That's true. You have explained that to me." Undeterred, he takes my hand and helps me to my feet.

My body trembles at his touch. My brain catches fire. What is happening to me? I am confused. Dazed. My world is coming apart from meeting Heraclius. Nothing in my life, or in my studies has ever prepared me for this momentous, inexplicable, life-changing event.

"I will be here waiting in your cave for you tomorrow when the sun is high overhead," he declares.

How can he be so certain? So unruffled? As if he is asking me if I want another helping of roasted spring lamb. An ordinary statement with extraordinary ramifications. Or is he a hallucination from the god? "I don't know," I mutter somewhat incoherently.

"You don't know if I'll be here tomorrow? Or if you will be here tomorrow?"

"I don't know!" I exclaim and run out of the cave, heading home, tightly clutching my scroll. Heraclius doesn't follow me, for which I am grateful. When I arrive at my destination, I dash into my room and fling myself on my mattress. I can hardly breathe. Remembering his touch on my hand. "Oh, Apollo," I murmur out loud. "Help me!"

I can hear the god's voice. "You have seen this man in visions, Selene. That is why you recognize him."

Visions? What visions? Why do I not remember?

That night I have difficulty sleeping. When I do slumber my dreams are disturbing. Apollo holds my hand, relaying messages I can't decipher. The nature god Pan dances with me in densely forested woods, far beyond. Parnassus. My mother Xanthippe watches me carouse in my fantasy state, an unforgiving look on her face.

I wake just before dawn. Roosters have been crowing in numerous village chicken yards, instructing hens to arise and lay in their nests. The hens cluck in response, ambling from their henhouses, pecking in the dirt, waiting their turns to lay their eggs in their favorite nesting spots in wooden fenced enclosures. Only after all of them have laid will gates be opened, freeing them to wander through the village, thus preventing eggs from being laid in unfavorable places. These birds are clever, as they instinctively know which yards and nests to return to when it is time to sleep.

Demetria has already risen. I hear her moving about in our little kitchen. I arise and put a light *chlamys* around my shoulders, the air still chill at this altitude. Once the sun has risen, the day will heat up quickly and become unbearable. I pull the quilt up over my mattress on its wooden platform, plump my small pillow, and go greet my grandmother.

"Selene!" she exclaims, giving me a quick hug. "You are up very early."

I blush in response, but she has turned away and doesn't notice. "We have feta cheese, dried figs, and olives to break our fast. And some left over pita bread, too. Kleida will be here later with our main meal. She is such a marvelous cook. We are lucky indeed."

"What time do you think that would be?" I inquire feigning naïveté.

"Dear one, you know what time that is. As the sun begins to set, when the heat of the day is diminishing," she replies, slicing the pita into bite-sized pieces on a wooden board with a dull knife.

"So we will not eat when the Apollo's Chariot is at its zenith?"

"At that time we will eat cold food left over from yesterday. As is our custom. Is there something wrong? Why do you ask questions for which you know the answers?"

"Oh, grandmother. I am simply inquiring." Guilt blossoms on my face, streaking down my neck, and ending at my reddened chest. Should I tell her? Or keep the secret to myself? Do I dare meet Heraclius at my cave? Although I had studied great poets, philosophers, and historians, they have no advice to resolve my present quandary.

"Here. Sit. I will serve you." She hands me a small woven bowl with a variety of foods in it.

I do as instructed.

"Mother, you pamper her too much," complains Xanthippe, walking quietly into the kitchen, yawning as she does so.

"As I did with you, too," Demetria gently reminds her.

"Umm hmmm," is mama's answer. "Too early for quarreling." She sits on a stool near the wooden table used for preparing food as well as dining. "You're right though. You're always right," she continues with barely-disguised sarcasm. She helps herself to a handful of dried figs and shovels them into her mouth. "So delicious," she murmurs. Xanthippe is putting on a little weight around her waist. "Selene," she turns to me.

"Yes, mama."

"I have awakened with my bleeding time this morning. You should be prepared. You know we always start on the same day."

"Oh," I gasp. "I didn't realize it is that time again. Do we have the cloths ready?"

"Yes. They are in the basket over there. Portia laundered them and folded them for us." She collects a few, handing several to me, along with a cord to fasten around my waist. As she passes by, she curiously reaches out to touch my breast. "Daughter. Your breasts are developing."

Embarrassed, I refrain from answering her spontaneous remark. Then pain spasms in my groin. The women's curse is ill-timed for my meeting at the cave today. I go to my chamber and arrange the cord and cloth and loosely arrange my *peplos* over it. Often on the first day of menarche I have discomfort and usually stay in bed. When Xanthippe is scheduled to be an outlet for Apollo during her woman's time, Demetria fills in for her as Pythia. A woman is not allowed to channel the god when she is bleeding.

But today... I simply cannot have my moon time today of all days!

Xanthippe does not experience the cramping pain that I have. "It's because I had a child," she has explained to me.

I return to the table to eat, but am not hungry. So I go to my mattress and lay down, restless.

The house grows hot as the sun is nearing its apex. Impulsively I make a decision. I will hike to the cave anyway. Bring some extra cloths with me. Beseech Apollo to assist. I quietly tiptoe through the house. Xanthippe is nowhere to be seen while Demetria is working at the horizontal loom moving the shuttle back and forth, creating cloth out of thread.

Hurrying up the mountain slope, I am out of breath when I get to the cave. It is empty. I make myself comfortable on the couch-stone cushion. Has Heraclius been here already and left? Did he come at all? I have no way of knowing. I wait. And wait. Excitement and concern turn to displeasure. Blood trickles down my legs. I change the cloth before I head down the mountain path towards home.

When I have accomplished that task, folding up the bloodied cloth to take home with me for Portia to launder, I hear a step on the gravel outside. Is it him at last?

"Oh, there you are," Heraclius remarks casually, as if our meeting is nothing out of the ordinary, as though people always meet in a deserted cave on a steep mountainside. He is dressed in the same short fustanella as yesterday with leather-thronged sandals on his feet, barechested as before.

"I have been waiting for you," I reproach him. Embarrassed, I make sure the stained cloth is well-hidden from view. I pull the *peplos* over my thighs as I sit on the cushion.

"I couldn't get here any faster," he replies, then lounges nonchalantly upon the couch-stone cushion next to me.

I am filled with relief, anger, and jealousy, too. Something or someone has delayed him. Our meeting appears to have little significance to him, unlike my own feelings of intensely fated destiny and longing. Perhaps I am simply desperate for companionship, as I have none. "You said noon," I continue, scolding him.

"Yes, I did. I am tardy." Heraclius then proceeds with a long discourse about his training. The Pythian Games. The crowds who have begun to gather for the event. None of that interests me because I have nothing with which to associate his descriptions, except several scrolls I have read.

I would like a heart-felt apology, but perceive it will not be forth-coming. Or preferably a declaration of love. I am uncomfortable with my moon time and want to leave, to wash up at home, and rest myself on my mattress. Yet he continues his monologue.

"My sponsor Aegeus has paid for my training, which includes..."

I perk up. "Aegeus is the merchant who brought delicious fish, octopus and spices as offerings to the Oracle."

He leans suggestively close to me. His breath tickles my ear. "I am sure you are correct," he whispers. "Aegeus is a big-hearted man."

Torn with mixed emotions, I can't make up my mind to stay or leave. Although dangerous and improper to stay in his company, I am attracted to the young man. Heraclius is beautiful in a reckless sort of way, like an untamed animal, stretched out languidly like a leopard on the rock cushion. Heraclius is self-absorbed and reminds me of the tale I read of Narcissus, a hunter from Boeotia, who became infatuated with his own image in a pool. I can't take my eyes off him. His gleaming expanse of skin smeared with olive oil beckons my touch.

To refrain from doing so, I argue with myself. Years of training and warnings whirl around in my mind like a dust devil on a hot day. If only I had some experience in order to determine what to do. Perhaps I can talk with Demetria about him. But she might be disappointed with me, which I couldn't bear. I have already hurt her once.

Being isolated from village life is not helpful. If I could talk with other young girls, they might advise me. All I've ever known is four women treating me as a baby, shielding me from the real world, the world of men. Worse yet, protecting me so that I will grow up to be the Pythia my family wishes me to be. A delicate flower not to be exposed to the blistering sun of the outside world.

Heraclius has stopped talking and is staring at me. I haven't noticed, so occupied am I with my thoughts and inner struggle.

"Selene," he says softly.

Startled out of my reverie, I reply, "Yes. I'm here."

"I wasn't certain. You have a faraway look in your eyes."

"I was contemplating."

"I've never known a girl who did such a thing as contemplate. I, myself, seldom do so," he continues proudly.

I am not sure if his comment is meant to be an insult or a compliment. How does he often befuddle my mind and my feelings? "Perhaps I should be going," I reply, not knowing what else to do but flee again.

"Stay just a little longer," he implores. "Selene, you're a strange girl. Unlike any I've known. Not that I've known many," he adds hastily, and changes the subject. "Do you like me?"

"Well, yes, I do. I shouldn't. But I do," I redden unexpectedly.

He sighs in relief. "Oh, that's good. I like you too, even if you are unearthly at times."

"Do you think so?"

"Um hm," he answers. "Don't you know that about yourself?"

"No one has ever told me so. My grandmother and my mother are similar to me, so I suppose we are all three strange. Maybe that is a requirement of being called to serve Apollo here at Delphi."

"Hmmm," he responds. "Perhaps if I kiss you, you will come down to earth."

"What!" I exclaim. "No, that can never be."

"I don't know why not. I like you. You like me. What could be more natural?"

"I can't. I mustn't. I shouldn't," I cry out and jump to my feet. "I'm to become the next Oracle. My mother and grandmother, the village, the world expects me to be a Pythia. I am not allowed. I don't dare violate Apollo. He would know. Then I will bring shame upon myself and everyone else. This is my life, just as yours is athletic competition and the Games," I try to explain.

"You're being difficult," he complains. "I don't know why I bother with you anyway. You're just a girl, even if you are to be the next Oracle. Girls are all alike. Unstable and moody, not to be trusted." He frowns.

I cannot tolerate him regarding me with scorn. "No, you're wrong! I am not difficult. You don't understand what I have been trained for. What a problem it is to be here with you. I would be an outcast if anyone knew."

"Really. An outcast? That's astonishing for one little kiss," he sulks.

"All right," I relent, afraid that he will leave and never return. "One kiss then."

Heraclius stands facing me. He is much taller than me and bundles me into his arms as if I was a little lamb. A lamb to the slaughter? Before I can think about the implications of that idea, he kisses me on my mouth. His lips are soft. Fleshy. Warm. I want that kiss to continue forever. Oh, gods, what is happening? What does it mean? Why can't I stop him? Why don't I want to stop him?

"Selene," he murmurs tenderly, as he breaks contact with my lips. He pulls me tighter to his chest. His heart is hammering against me. Then Heraclius kisses my face, my throat, my shoulder. I sense a huge swelling under his skirt. Nothing could prepare me for the abrupt change in his male anatomy.

The cave swirls around me. My life transforms in that instant. "For years I fantasized that I would forgo the privilege of becoming an Oracle. To have a husband and a family. To live a normal life outside the constraints and responsibilities of Delphi. To be free. Here is my chance. We can be together as husband and wife."

Ignoring my impassioned speech, he slides his hand over my *peplos* to feel my maturing breasts, as I experience an unfamiliar rush of energy. Like rainfall inundating the slopes of Mt. Parnassus, flooding the valley below.

Then I remember my moon time and stop his exploring hand. "Not today, Heraclius. I cannot."

He groans in frustration. "Selene…"

"I am going now," I tell him, mustering strength from somewhere inside myself, pulling myself away from his embrace and rearranging my *peplos*.

"Are you a virgin?" he asks.

"Of course. What else would I be?"

"Is that why…?"

This is my opportunity to leave, to hurry down the mountain to the safety of home.

I hear his mournful voice behind me. "Selene! Please come back!" His voice echoes, pursuing me down the path.

Chapter 5

DEMETRIA   AGE 15   435 BC

Shame can be stronger than love. For interminable days and nights I remain at home with my studies, avoiding the cave until the Pythian Games are finished, when participants and spectators leave. I cannot return until I know I will not meet Heraclius again, as I doubt I could control myself a second time.

One night after supper Demetria comes to my bedchamber. I am sitting on my mattress reading the most recent scroll loaned to us from a wealthy pilgrim, a volume of history by Herodotus.

"Selene. You are very quiet lately. You hardly leave the house. You read all day long. Sometimes I hear you cry after you've gone to bed." She sits down next to me on the thin mattress covering the wooden frame. "My darling Selene. What is wrong? Tell me."

I have withheld my secrets by sheer willpower, but grandmother's tenderness releases them. "Grandmama. I must declare to you..." My voice breaks and I tremble. After I regain control of myself, I relate the whole story to her. Finding the cave and making it into a second home. Apollo's visits and our conversations. Studying on my own in my rocky sanctuary. Finally my experiences with Heraclius. "I am ashamed."

"My darling. There is no reason for shame. You are a girl. A young inexperienced girl cut off from ordinary life, forced to live an abnormal existence. Your mother and me, we are the ones who deserve censure. We isolated you here with us, believing we were doing the correct thing. To protect you from harm. To train you with excellence, better than we had been. For you to become a finer Oracle than we could ever hope to be."

I cling to the old woman, her words reassuring and comforting. "I'm grateful to you dear grandmother."

"We are proud of you, Selene. I had no idea that Apollo was already schooling you. I should have known."

"Grandmother, can you forgive me?"

"There's nothing to forgive, child. Your mother and I work at Apollo's Temple here at Delphi, acting as intermediaries for the god and his prophecies. We are not gods, but imperfect. Human and thus fragile."

"I am afraid to see Heraclius again. I have no restraint over myself. I would behave with dishonor."

"I understand my dear one. But your feelings are natural."

"How can you say that?"

"Because I once loved a man."

"You did?" I have never heard the story.

"Your grandfather. He was a priest of Apollo here at Delphi, older than me. I met him when we performed the rituals for Apollo at the Temple sanctuary. As Priest of Apollo he interpreted my messages for pilgrims and translated those into poetry. He was highly intelligent, as well as talented in verse and rhyme. He was intense and excitable and loved me, in his fashion."

I relax, listening to her mesmerizing story.

"We struggled in vain against our feelings, but eventually lost that battle. We then met secretly wherever we could, usually late at night when everyone was asleep. We had intimate relations. I stopped taking the herb *silphium* because I aspired to have his child, foolishly believing we could marry. He seeded my body with your mother. During my pregnancy I was hidden away in a nearby village while another woman took my place as Pythia. The new Oracle was ineffective, quite disappointing and sometimes disastrously wrong."

I take her hand, deeply touched, listening to the story of her life.

"Your grandfather was removed to the Temple of Apollo at Corinth and I never saw him again. Yet he influenced wealthy men who made pilgrimages to Delphi. Thus before Xanthippe was born, this white house was built and furnished for us so that we could live here without care. On the condition that I wouldn't reveal his identity. I never have." She smiled to herself. "I have honored his and others' wishes."

I squeeze her hand.

"I supposed I would be the Delphic Oracle until I died. Yet within time I could tell that Xanthippe had the gift of prophecy as I did. However, she took after her father, was disobedient and strong-willed. I loved her as best as I could, but it was never enough. She wanted to become a midwife and bring new life into the world, but that plan was rejected by others. In her rebellion she had a child. You, Selene."

Her story is breathtaking. As dramatic as Aeschylus' plays. As heartbreaking as life. The old woman had remained loving and loyal throughout decades.

"I will teach you whatever else you need to know about being an Oracle."

"Perhaps that is not necessary. I talk with Apollo nearly every day."

"You do? That is astonishing. Perhaps prophetic endowment of our family has grown stronger through several generations, ending with you."

I flush. "I am not that talented, grandmama."

"How can you say that? I never sat in a cave and had discussions with Apollo. As far as I know neither has Xanthippe."

"I just assumed…" I begin.

"Yes, but your assumption is mistaken, dear heart," she interrupts soothingly. "You have abilities far beyond anything I've known or heard about. Perhaps your mother and I were correct in how we raised you. Maybe you will become the greatest Oracle of Delphi."

These auspicious words coming from the woman I love most in this world unnerves me to my core. "Thank you, dearest grandmama. I hope I can live up to your expectations."

She answers back. "You already do, my darling."

"But...what about Heraclius?"

"Oh, yes. Heraclius. Hmmm," she murmurs. "You must now take the sacred herb *silphium* every day for protection in case you become intimate with him. I have no prophetic words to offer you, child. Perhaps your relationship is for you and Apollo to decipher. Possibly there is a special characteristic that Apollo is training you for, beyond our puny mortal viewpoint."

As Demetria pronounces this fateful message to me, gooseflesh rises on my skin. I have learned to recognize those as validation permeating through my body. "Truth bumps," I declare.

Grandmother continues. "By the way, the Pythian games have concluded," she offers.

"Then I can return to my cave as before."

"Yes," she agrees. "I think your time in the cave with Apollo is significant. But remember to take the herb. Every day without fail."

"Yes, I will."

Early the next morning I quickly dress, eat, grab a scroll I have been studying, and head to my cave. I haven't felt so carefree since my last experience in the cave with Heraclius. How can I love him and yet be frightened at the same time? Perhaps Apollo might have an answer.

When I arrive I observe a disturbance in my rocky haven. The stone-couch cushion is lying on the floor, the top partially shredded, while excrement from a wild animal is heaped in a corner. I didn't think to bring the broom or anything to clean with, so I will have to accept the destruction for now. Although the cushion is torn on one side, I replace it on the stone-couch with the reverse side up, lay the scroll next to it, and sit down, trembling.

I am filled with dread. Is the animal coming back? Am I in danger?

Apollo is instantly at my ear, urging me to listen. "Trouble in the Greek world is affirmed," he utters. "Athenians will ban Megarians from markets and harbors of Athens. The Peloponnesian League is certain to take revenge over this action. The question is when will this happen and what form will it take?"

Because of my study of maps, I know where Athens is located. Many pilgrims travel from Athens and its neighbors to Delphi. Athens is by far the largest and richest city-state in Greece, three times the size of Corinth. Treasure from Delos, another sacred temple of Apollo, was moved to Athens some 20 years before. The port and military harbor at Piraeus, safeguarding Athens by long walls, has now been closed to Megara, the area directly to the west of Athens. This closure will hamper Megara's ability to ship and trade goods. The Athenian fleet, containing hundreds of *triremes*, protected at the harbor at Piraeus, can now be viewed as a menace to Megara and thus to Sparta.

This Decree could also affect Delphi, as the Isthmus of Corinth will be blocked. Pilgrims will not be able to trek over the Megarian plain, but instead to Mount Garenea, and travel over an extremely difficult mountain pass to reach the Temple. Why would Athens repulse Megara and thereby insult the Peloponnesian League? I knew from reading Herodotus that war-like Sparta and others of the League will be righteously angered over the Megarian decree. Their response might be to attack Athens, which contains vast treasures that are valuable as spoils of war.

As I sit contemplating on my stone-couch, I can sense the enormous ramifications that Apollo is conveying. Is this what being an Oracle entails? Does Apollo warn of current dangers as well as future ones? Since I have never been part of the ancient ritual in the *Adyton*, I have no idea. I need to talk to Demetria. She would know. Embracing the precious scroll as well as the valuable information from Apollo, I hurry down the mountain path.

I rush into our extraordinary little house, one I now know was constructed of Eros, built for a woman by her lover. A Delphic Priest, a Delphic Oracle, and their child were joined in that sacred venture.

"Grandmother!" I shout.

"What is it, Selene?" my mother Xanthippe utters, poking her head out from her chamber.

"Where is grandmama?" I question her.

"She is napping. Can I help you with something? You seem terribly upset."

"Apollo…Megara…Sparta…war," I pant breathlessly. "Something terrible is happening or about to happen."

"Slow down, daughter. I can't understand you. Here is some water." She hands me a cup half full.

I gulp it quickly then continue. "Mother. I received a message from Apollo. A vital message. My first one. Well, not the first, but the most notable."

Xanthippe sits on a portable stool and urges me to do the same.

I can hardly breathe.

"You received a message from Apollo? Today?"

"Yes. I was... in my cave."

"What cave?"

"The cave where I take my scrolls to study. Oh, mother. Too many details to tell you."

Demetria comes into the room, awakened by the commotion. "Selene. Xanthippe. What is happening? I heard anxious voices."

I jump up and run to her. "Grandmother. I had my first truly important message from Apollo! Just now. Well, a little while ago. In my cave."

"Go on, child. What did he say?"

"Athens has closed their port and markets to Megara."

"Athens and Megara? Aren't they close neighbors?" Demetria inquires.

Xanthippe sits quietly, trying to understand, but not totally following the discussion.

"Yes. Megara is part of the Peloponnesian League. The League will mostly likely be offended by Athens and the Decree. This could lead to war."

"The League was formed by Sparta," Demetria comments with alarm. She is also knowledgeable about history and geography.

"That is exactly what I am trying to say."

"Apollo told you this."

"Yes."

"You didn't ask him any questions first?"

"No. He began to talk after I got to the cave. Some wild animal had caused disorder in my absence."

"The god's news is cause for concern. When did this action with Megara take place?"

"I don't know. He hasn't told me that part."

"I need to send word. But to whom? And by what means? Everyone may have returned home from the Games. I'm not sure if the Priest is still in residence." Demetria looks distressed.

"Do you want me to ask Apollo for more information?" I ask.

"You are able ask Apollo for information without being at the sanctuary in a trance?" Xanthippe questions in astonishment.

"Yes, Selene, if you could," continues Demetria, ignoring her daughter for the moment. "That would be helpful."

I am used to the quiet of my cave and a calmness while I am there. I have neither quiet nor calm at this moment. "I will try."

Xanthippe speaks up. "Would one of you please explain?"

"Not now, daughter," challenges Demetria. "You must wait."

"Hmmp," Xanthippe retorts.

"I don't know what to do, Selene," Demetria murmurs. "I've never experienced Apollo outside the formal ritual."

"Let us be quiet." Initially I hear nothing, feel nothing.

Xanthippe interjects a valuable comment. "There is a group of Athenian *hoplite* soldiers with their commander billeted near the village and some cavalry, too."

"How do you know?" queries Demetria.

Xanthippe shrugs her shoulders as an answer. "Do you want me to tell their commander?"

"In a moment. Let us see if Apollo has any further information for us," responds her mother.

"Very well."

I calm myself. I discern vague murmurings in my head but nothing I can clearly decipher. "What else can you tell me about Athens and Megara?" I entreat the god.

"In 10 days," Apollo speaks.

"This will happen 10 days from now?"

"Yes," the god answers succinctly.

"So there is time."

"There is no time. All has been accomplished except the actual Megarian Decree itself. This action has been planned for at least a season and will be voted on and easily passed."

"Is there anything that can be altered?" I ask.

"No," responds Apollo. "Athens' power is growing and so is her impertinent *hybris*, especially since winning the war against the Persians. The Spartans are furious with Athens gaining supremacy in Greece."

As I repeat the god's statements, terrible premonitions run through my body, tightening my upper abdomen into a knot of apprehension. "Grandmother. I'm afraid."

"Let me talk to the Commander," Xanthippe speaks with authority to the two of us, taking charge.

"Is there a Priest in residence?" asks Demetria.

"Not at this time," rejoins my mother.

"Then, yes," reacts Demetria. "Bring the Commander here so that we can fully explain. He may want to take action."

"Here? To our house!?" Xanthippe exclaims.

"What Apollo has said is significant. I want no information lost or garbled in our communication with him. Bringing the Commander here is appropriate for this solemn circumstance."

"Very well," and she leaves.

"Sit, Selene. We must collect our thoughts while we wait," and she relaxes on a stool in the *oikos*, the common room.

In my studies I had read the expression "Time stood still." Was it in a poem? Or a play? Yet I understand its significance as we wait impatiently for Xanthippe to return with the Commander.

Kleida has not showed up with our supper and I am hungry. I wander to the kitchen to see if we have any food. I find a hard-boiled egg, pita bread, and figs and start to eat them in my nervousness. Before I finish I hear a commotion in the *oikos*, stop what I'm doing, and hurry out there.

Xanthippe ushers in Commander Sophus of Acharnae. As on official business, he is wearing his breastplate and leg armor, called greaves, while carrying his Corinthian helmet under his arm, red *chlamys* draped over his shoulders.

She introduces all of us to him. "This is my mother Demetria. Over here is Selene who received the messages."

He nods. He glances furtively at Xanthippe, who ignores him. They know each other, I am sure. Even a blind King Oedipus could see that.

"Revered Pythia," he calls Xanthippe by her sacred title, "let me hear the messages from Apollo."

"Selene has heard the messages." She addresses me. "Tell Sophus what you heard."

I feel flustered and timid but recite all the information to the *hoplite* Commander that I can remember.

Commander Sophus' face darkens into a contemptuous scowl as he listens to my words but says nothing.

"Did I forget any details?" I ask my grandmother.

"No, you have done well, my dear."

Sophus speaks heatedly. "Accursed Megarians. What have they done now to provoke such an edict from Athens? Those scheming Spartans with their Peloponnesian allies, always stirring up trouble. They are little more than barbarians, or Persians, not like real Greeks at all."

I am distressed by his statements. In my opinion, he has overlooked the essentials of Apollo's message entirely. Does he not understand history? Is he blinded to everything except settling of old scores? In my status as a submissive woman, I am not entitled to discuss, disagree, or argue with him. I stand silently fuming.

Sophus turns to my mother while ignoring me. "Thank you for the information, Xan....I mean worthy Pythia." He grimaces at his error. "My men and I will leave for Athens at first light, to inform Pericles and his delegate Timon. If what Apollo reveals is true, I must not hesitate." Sophus leaves brusquely without a farewell.

We are lowly women, after all, not worthy of a parting remark. Or is he simply embarrassed?

Apollo has sent my first significant dispatch. I am not certain of the outcome but have an awful feeling inside. Is this often the case of misinterpretation, like the story Xanthippe told me of King Croesus? Does a questioner have a particular outcome in mind and ignores all other possibilities? Only Apollo knows.

Chapter 6

POSEIDON'S BOY   AGE 16   434 BC

The three of us in our little house are essentially cut off from the outside world. Thus we do not know what meaning Apollo's message conveys, nor what events are developing in Athens, Corinth, Argos, Sparta, or Thebes. These and other city-states exist isolated from each other between mountains and oceans, without connecting plains as in other countries.

Xanthippe's functioning as Pythia can discern external events from the questions of pilgrims, who are flocking to Delphi demanding answers. However, she isn't sharing her insights with either grandmother or me.

Once a month if Xanthippe is unable to perform her oracular duties Demetria takes over for her. My grandmother can then obtain clues to the happenings in Greece based on questions posed to her while seated on Apollo's throne in the *Adyton*. Many months go by while the two of us anxiously await the opportunity.

Finally Demetria is able to behave as a stand-in to Pythia. She comes home from the lengthy Oracular event, still somewhat intoxicated from the Delphic fumes, but eager to tell me what she has gleaned.

"You heard Apollo rightly long ago," she begins. "There are continuing threats of war from both sides. Sparta declares that Athens has insulted the Peloponnesian League. Athens claims Sparta wants to take control of Greece. Corinth fought with Corcyra over control of Epidamnus. Corinth was defeated at the last moment by Athenians fighting on the side of Corcyra. Hatred then exploded from Corinth towards Athens, while skirmishes erupt periodically from participants in various city-states. Old jealousies are breaking out with violence. Yet all parties are striving to avoid destroying the Thirty Years Peace Treaty."

"Oh, gods, what will happen next?"

"I don't know," reacts the old lady. "Sparta voted decisively by who shouted the loudest, as is their custom, determining that Athens violated the Treaty. The Spartans are coming here to Delphi to consult with Xanthippe or me, depending on her moon time."

"Then all sides are angry and blaming each other."

"Unfortunately that is the case. What does Apollo say, Selene? Is he talking to you?"

"Nothing coherent. First I hear mutterings and mumblings followed by screams, as if I am listening to groups of men dying in mortal combat. Women wail. Then I have visions, which is unusual for me. I see men stabbing each other. Blood spurts. Ships in sea battles catch fire and sink. One side, then the other, declare victory. Then the tide turns as victors became losers, then losers become victorious. The sights Apollo shares with me are one great hodgepodge of destruction and death. I cannot make sense of it. It gives me nightmares." I shudder. "What questions did you hear today?"

Demetria sighs, my story aligning with her experiences. "Pilgrims from all over Greece request answers similar to your visions:

"Is my son alive?

Will there be enough food for the winter?

Shall I send my slaves to fight on our behalf?

Who will win the upcoming siege?"

Where will we be safe?"

She laments. "I'm melancholic, Selene. When I was a young Oracle, during war with the Persians, pilgrims wanted resolutions to these same sorts of troubled questions."

Just then Kleida appears with supper, holding the earthenware pot with thick cloths to prevent burning her hands. "*Kotopoulo* again tonight!" she announces cheerfully. She is a welcome visitor, not just for the delicious chicken she is bringing, but also for her buoyant nature, a relief to this troubling day. She places the pot on the kitchen table and opens the lid. Steam gushes out while the pleasurable smell of baked chicken fills the room.

"It's an old chicken but should be tasty. You see how it's falling off the bone? I have baked it all day with the last of the rice from the Athenian merchant Aegeus."

"May the gods bless that man," declares Demetria.

"I wonder if we will be able to get more rice anytime soon." I look knowingly at my grandmother.

"Let's eat," declares Demetria, changing the subject. She asks Kleida, "Have you seen my daughter?"

"Not today," replies the thin, energetic woman, with stringy muscles on arms and legs, tough as an old goat. "I will let her know that I have brought supper if I do see her."

"Thank you," says Demetria graciously. She removes three wooden bowls from the open cupboard, collects three spoons, and places all those on the inside table, as the house has cooled off from the heat of the day.

"Would you like me to cut up the chicken?" asks Kleida.

"Thank you, no, Kleida. We should be able to do so ourselves."

"Enjoy your dinner, then. I'll be back later to collect the pot."

I get out our old carving knife and easily cut the chicken into pieces, ladling the meat and broth into bowls. I spoon some cooked rice along with chicken into them for my grandmother, and then some for myself. We eat in edgy silence.

Before we finish our meal, Xanthippe strolls casually into our small kitchen. "Smells wonderful," she announces, helps herself to the food, and sits. Mother doesn't notice the tense atmosphere but eats with gusto, periodically licking her fingers. The three of us finish the whole pot, except for a single chicken leg.

Xanthippe happily announces. "Participants for the Olympic Games will be coming soon to begin their training. Then two weeks later athletes will journey to Olympus, spectators will arrive, and the Games will commence. A noteworthy athlete will light the Olympic torch on the altar of the sanctuary of Hestia in Olympia."

Demetria looks at me with sudden concern. "Are you still going to your cave every day?" she asks discreetly.

"Yes," I reply.

"Is that wise?" she questions.

"I'm not sure," I answer.

"You remember the incident of the wild animal in your cave?" She looks at me meaningfully.

"I have not forgotten."

"Take care. Remember the herb," she whispers.

"I take it daily."

I withdraw to my bedchamber to reflect and rest. No scrolls tonight. My mind races with exhausting visions and messages, then shifts to the Olympic Games. Heraclius may be in Delphi soon. Will he be the one selected to light the Olympic torch? Again I experience clashing emotions. Excitement at possibly seeing him. Fear of the power of my love towards him. My unruly body pulsating with a life of its own, like a ravenous beast.

Eros has been cruel, shooting his arrow into my gullible heart. Leaving me to bleed. Ah, yes. I love Heraclius. Poor unfortunate wretch that I am. A prisoner. Of my sex. Of my life. Of Delphi.

Then Apollo shows up in my chamber. "Selene," he says. "Despair not. A woman has no power. No property. No rights. All that is true. But you, Selene. You are different."

"How is that possible? I'm not even a woman. Still a girl."

"You above all others can hear my prophecies without need of the mind-altering fumes of the Sacred Cave."

"Apollo, I gave the Commander your messages but he ignored them. He heeds only what he wants to hear."

"Yet not all is lost. Some will hear the messages you pass on from me. Others will be saved. You have a mission, a sacred duty."

"I doubt that," I answer despondently.

"Do not question the gods. I bring you knowledge. Eventually wisdom. You are to be of service. Your life is a miracle."

"I do not understand, Apollo," I mutter to him. "You talk in riddles."

"You will comprehend in time, Selene. Meanwhile follow your heart. Trust my messages and your feelings. They will guide you truly, because you are my servant. Your feelings are my messages."

Like a mist Apollo dissolves into nothingness.

Obsessing about Heraclius I fall asleep, wondering what the god means.

"Selene." Grandmother is standing at the side of my bed.

Startled, I awaken with a start. "Grandmother, what is the matter?" The room is bright with the morning sun.

"I'm told the athletes and their sponsors arrived at Delphi last night, to commence training."

"Heraclius?"

"Yes, him too."

"Oh no!"

"I've changed my mind. I think you need to face your fears about him."

Is Demetria in league with Apollo? Did he speak to her last night as well as to me? Trust your feelings because they are my messages. "Very well, grandmama."

"Here is the chicken leg from last night and some yogurt. I've mixed the *silphium* with some water. Drink. Then eat quickly and go to your cave."

Wordlessly I do as she instructs. She practically pushes me out through the open doorway.

I follow the winding Sacred Way then trudge up the hill. What or who would I encounter? My feelings are Apollo's messages.

I observe the exquisite marble statues along the way. Greeks have veneration for the human form, revealed in statues and vases. I idolize Heraclius' body. The ripple of his muscles. His lips that I long to kiss. I worship and cherish him. I love him beyond all reason and logic. I shouldn't but I do. I cannot help myself.

The morning is sunny, but still cool. The entrance to the cave is just ahead. I'm not wearing my *himation* and I shiver.

I peek in. Heraclius is waiting for me!

"Selene!" he exclaims. He rushes to me, wraps his strong arms around me, and holds me tightly. "I've been praying to Apollo all night. To have him bring you to me. I hurried up the mountain as soon as it was light."

I stroke the muscle of his left arm, the veins standing out in visible blue traces. "Apollo heard you," I murmur.

"What?"

"Never mind. I'm here now."

"I love you. I have missed you terribly. Nothing matters except you."

"Not even the Games?"

"Well, perhaps those. But they pale in comparison to your lapis eyes." He bends over and kisses me fully on the mouth. "Your fair hair," he murmurs into my ear.

I have dreamt endlessly of this moment and return his kiss with the full force of my feelings for him, embracing him tightly. Shamelessly. Unabashedly. At home at last in his arms. Gorging myself on his affection. Nothing to fear any longer.

"Trust your feelings. They are my messages."

He eagerly removes my *peplos*. He unfastens his leather waistband and his skirt slides to the ground. Naked as I am. He is fully erect, the tip of his penis peeking through the foreskin.

"I love you, Heraclius," I tell him, gazing into his eyes. They could startlingly change shades from tones of the profound green of a deep pond to iridescent as when one stares into that same pond with sunlight shining on the surface.

He wordlessly removes the cushion then stands me on the solid couch-stone. He is extremely tall. With me on the stone, his mouth is level with my breasts. He kisses and licks the nipples. Moves to my mound. His tongue waggles at the opening. Pleasure bursts through me.

"Are you a virgin?" he asks for the second time.

"Yes," I reply simply.

"I will be very sensitive with you." He spits into his palm, applies it to his erection. Then he gently eases himself into me.

I feel my maidenhead tear and some blood leaks out.

"I love you, Selene!" he exclaims, his words reverberating through the cave.

There is no pain. I feel only ecstasy and joy, as Sappho has described.

"Love shook my heart
like wind pounding mountain oaks."

He roars gutturally, the sound coming from deep within his throat. "I love you!" he cries again.

Within moments I feel the spurt of his semen into me. His body sags allowing his penis to slide out of me. He picks up the cushion, replacing it on the couch-stone, sits, and pulls me onto his lap, my head resting in the hollow of his chest, his arm around me, cradling me. "I'm sorry," he mumbles. "I should have pulled out sooner."

"It is fine," I speak against his chest. "I take an herb to prevent pregnancy."

"That is reassuring."

We cuddle quietly. The feel of his skin on my body is the most delicious sensation I have ever yet experienced in my short life, as though we have become one person.

His body jerks. "Um. Selene. Will you marry me?" he sleepily requests.

"What?" I giggle at his question.

But he is already snoring, sitting upright.

I am afraid we might tumble off the couch-stone and hurt ourselves. "Heraclius!" I say softly.

"Mmphhh," he snorts. "What is it?"

"You are falling asleep. I don't want us to collapse to the ground."

"Oh, you're right." He looks around. "We need a more suitable place than this in the future."

"That's true," and I giggle again.

"I will explore the area for some grass to lay on. Or I can bring my sleeping roll next time."

"Next time," I echo.

He yawns and stretches himself. Heraclius is a fabulous specimen. The years of his physical training are evident in every inch of his body. His face is handsome, too. I am honored to be with him. But how can I be with him? Delphi and the Oracle stand in our way.

"I am going, Selene," he announces unexpectedly. "I must attend training. I will be missed."

"Now? When can I see you again?"

"I'm not sure."

Confusion spins around me again. "I don't understand. You just told me you love me. You asked to marry me."

"I did?"

"Yes."

"You must have heard me incorrectly. Perhaps you are having a fantasy from Apollo."

"No, Heraclius. I heard you quite distinctly." My irritation begins to smolder.

"I must go." He pulls on his skirt and fastens it, although remarkably he is still wearing his sandals. He kisses me quickly and leaves me standing with my mouth agape, naked in my chilled cave, unable to reconcile his words with his actions. I feel as though we are torn apart in that moment. My tattered soul thirsts to follows him.

Apollo, my feelings are your messages. I am bewildered. Heraclius must swim in the murky deep with the watery god Poseidon, messenger of confusion, illusion, and delusion.

I dress quickly then shuffle down the mountain path. Heraclius has wounded me. I carefully watch my faltering steps on the rocks and pebbles.

When I return home, to assuage my hurt feelings, I decide to write my first words of poetry. For years I have been well-schooled in poetry, plays, and philosophy. I am usually too embarrassed to try a clumsy attempt to emulate wise men and women who are leagues beyond me.

Then Sappho and her romantic words come to mind, and I gain courage. I tear off a small piece from a shabby scroll of blank papyrus and use a hard reed for writing, dipped in ink made from charcoal mixed with a little water. And write, as I often do for my lessons. I entitle my composition "Poseidon's Boy," named for the mysterious god of the watery depths.

Poseidon's Boy by Selene of Delphi
Now I see you.

Then you are gone.
A fish tail
Swishes into the deep
unknown
mysterious
unfocused
currents.
Alive with pathos and humor
I cannot hold your shadow.
You are everywhere
and nowhere
Swimming two directions at once
Promising
Forgetting.
Loving
Offending.
Babbling words from a Greek chorus.
Insults disguised as comedy.
Comedy veiled as caring.
Lost
In illusions.
There is no stable location where you exist.
All is mistiness and reflections
in mirrored pools
and smoke from cooking fires.
Now I perceive you.
Then you are someone else.
Somewhere else
beyond mountains and oceans.
Soaring like a hawk in the breeze
of non-existent wind.

A wavering mirage on a sultry day.
Fish hooks can't catch you.
Neither can my love.

The Muses have offered me words to describe Heraclius and our per-plexing relationship. After the ink dries, I fold the scrap and hide it under my mattress. I don't want anyone to read it. The words are too revealing. Yet amazingly the writing has soothed my spirit. I take note of the after-effect and thank the Nine Sisters.

My poem reminds me of Bacchylides, whose words I would find years later in a scroll:

"To great Poseidon, seismic godhead, you were born
By Tithra, Troizen's shining queen—listen, look!—this splendid gold
Ring, adornment of my royal hand—dive down to where your father dwells,
Bold boy, and fetch it back from the marine abyss."

Chapter 7

XANTHIPPE   AGE 17   433 BC

By force of will and sheer obstinacy I stay away from my cave, struggling with myself. I cannot tolerate more heartbreak. I remain in my chamber much of the time, reading and contemplating. What can I do? Should I wait for Heraclius? Will he return? Am I but an inconsequential part of his eventful life? I adore him but to what end, except misery?

I have no answers. There is no one and nothing to consult except the scrolls. Sappho's words are a balm that assuages my mood:

"Immortal Aphrodite, daughter of Zeus, goddess
Of artful love-charms, weaver of wiles, I implore you,
Do not, mistress, overpower my heart
With distress and grief,
But come, if you have ever
Lent me your ear, hearing my voice
From afar and answered me."

Sappho has been in love. She too was overwhelmed with sadness and confusion. She speaks to me over time and distance to share her unhappiness. Perhaps I should commune with Aphrodite instead of Apollo. I am not interested in blockades and war and bloodshed. I only want to be comforted in Heraclius' arms. To know he loves me. To declare himself to me without subterfuge. To become his wife.

Suddenly I hear Apollo's voice. "Selene."

"Yes, Apollo. I am listening," but I am paying attention with only half a mind. I am distracted.

"A battle will commence soon. The Corinthian navy is at sea. Near Sybota. They are poised to fight against Corcyra and Athens."

I groan. "Not again. These visions of war are more than I can manage, Apollo. I have other pressing questions. Like what about Heraclius?"

"The athlete?"

"Yes. Him."

"He is unimportant in the larger scheme of the affairs of men."

"Not to me, Apollo," I implore. "Tell me what to do."

"You must pay attention to what I say, Selene. Many men will pay a high price. Their wives and children also. Cities and countries are at risk. Tell them, Selene. There is no time left."

"I cannot. I am only an ordinary woman. Not even an Oracle. Who will listen to me?"

"You must impart what I have told you."

"Tell who, Apollo?"

"Anyone who will listen."

I burst into tears. Beyond frustration. Beyond longing. "I have no voice. I am like Cassandra of Troy. No one paid her any heed either and great Troy was destroyed.

"Find your grandmother."

"Very well." I locate Demetria in the *gyneceum*. She head is resting on the loom, but her countenance is grey, eyes open and staring. I am instantly alarmed. "Grandmother." I shake her. She does not respond. "Demetria," I call her name. Still there is no answer or movement. I fear the worst.

I run to the doorway. "Mother," I cry out. "Mother. Where are you?" Xanthippe is nowhere to be seen.

I return to Demetria's side. I feel her hand. Cold and clammy. "No. No!" I exclaim. "You cannot leave me. Come back!" The day and timing is overwhelming me. I can do nothing but keen. In the scrolls I have read of women grieving over the death and destruction of their families and homes. The despair and grief I feel has no equal in literature. Those are merely empty words on papyrus.

The depths are awful, as if I am falling into a black chasm, alone and friendless. I am terrified at the events happening around me as well as the god's severe warning. Helpless to do anything or take any action. The sudden change in my life, losing my beloved grandmother, is agonizing.

"Heraclius!" I shout hysterically, as though he could hear me. I should go find him since he is at Delphi. I have no way of knowing his whereabouts, but want to try.

I kiss Demetria's cooling cheek, and place a *chlamys* covering her head. Then I ascend the familiar mountain path as quickly as I am able. When I arrive at the cave Heraclius is not there.

I just as swiftly descend the trail and return to my home. Xanthippe has not returned to our house while Demetria's body is stiffening. She has departed this world.

Although I have never been to Delphi village, I must take action. A well-worn trail leads there which I follow. When I get to the first dilapidated hovel, I hesitate. Chickens peck at the ground in front of the house while a billy goat is standing on his front two legs against a poplar tree, chewing on low hanging leaves. Who lives here? How will I be greeted? No one knows me by sight except Kleida and Portia. I go to the doorway and peer in. An unfamiliar woman looks back at me questioningly.

"Please forgive me for disturbing you, Lady. I am known as Selene, daughter of Xanthippe and granddaughter of Demetria."

"Oh, yes, please come in." She wipes her wet hands on her *chiton*. "I have heard of you and know your mother." She looks around.

"Please sit, Lady Selene," she points with embarrassment at a rickety wooden chair.

"I cannot. I have bad news and I need to find Xanthippe at once."

The woman is suddenly distressed. "Bad news?" she inquires.

"Yes, very bad news indeed. My grandmother Demetria is… I think she has died. I don't know what to do."

"Let us find your mother and we will sort this out." Rhoda, the village woman, takes charge.

I follow her wordlessly as she heads outdoors and makes her way to Kleida's cottage. The cook is standing at the outside earthen oven when we find her.

"Selene!" Kleida exclaims. "What in the world are you doing here?"

"I don't know where else to go."

"Oh, my dear girl. What is the matter?"

"Grandmother," I gulp anxiously. "There's something wrong with her. We need to find my mother."

"Of course, my dear. Of course." She pulls half-cooked food out of the stone oven and sets the pot on a nearby well-used wooden table. "It will burn otherwise." She rubs her cheek as she thinks of a plan.

I can hardly stand still with the tension and terror I am feeling. "And that's not all…" I want to tell her of Apollo's warning.

"Not now, Selene," she interrupts me. "Give me a moment to collect my thoughts." Then she exclaims, "There are some athletes holding an unofficial tournament in the *stadion*. Aegeus of Athens may be with them. He is a powerful and influential man. I'm sure he will have a suggestion of what we can do."

"Yes, Aegeus. He is the man who brought us food."

"That's the one."

"Heraclius' sponsor."

"Um, yes," the woman replies slowly, breaking eye contact. "His… sponsor. You wait here. I will go find Aegeus."

"No, I'm going with you."

"I don't think that's a good idea, Selene."

"Why not?"

"It's a long way."

"I'm used to walking long distances."

"Very well," assents Kleida reluctantly.

I have never been to the *stadion* and so closely follow Kleida.

A huge crowd has gathered there. I can hear cheering for various athletes.

As we grow closer to the *stadion*, I spot the veiled figure of Xanthippe, my mother, near the entrance. Although she is hidden by her clothing, I recognize her. She has her arms enfolded around an athlete's waist, a very tall athlete, while his arm is resting on her shoulder. They are nuzzling together.

Kleida tries to pull me in a different direction but I am instantly single-minded. As I get close I confirm that the man she is hugging is Heraclius.

"Heraclius!" I yell.

He turns to look at me, surprise and humiliation instantly written on his features. He quickly takes his arm off Xanthippe's shoulder who spins around to see what has interrupted them.

"Selene," she murmurs with astonishment.

"Yes, mother," as I walk up to her.

"What are you doing here?" The same question has been asked of me earlier, but with a different motive. "Excuse me, Heraclius," as she begs his pardon and turns to confront me. "Why aren't you home, Selene?"

"I could demand the same question of you," I retort angrily.

She nonchalantly waves my question away as if it is a bee buzzing round her.

"Grandmother," I continue relentlessly. "Something has happened to her."

Instantly Xanthippe is paying attention. For the first time she sees Kleida standing behind me, mortified and upset. "Demetria?" she inquires.

"Yes, mother. I think she has died." I am infuriated with her and Heraclius and am being malicious on purpose. "Hello, Heraclius," I disdainfully direct a greeting towards him.

Xanthippe looks at the two of us. "Do you know each other?" she queries with shock.

"Intimately," I reply. Suddenly I can understand his previous actions.

"What?" she exclaims. "Heraclius. Explain what she means," she demands of him.

"We have been lovers, mother," I interrupt harshly before Heraclius has a chance to concoct a lie. "He told me he loves me and asked me to marry him." I want to wound each of them as I am now suffering.

"Is that true?" my mother interrogates him furiously.

"Yes, in part it is true," the athlete admits grudgingly.

"Which part?" she says, hostility growing in her voice and manner. He shrugs, unwilling to reply.

"Come, Selene. Let us go home." She grabs my arm, turns abruptly and we hurriedly return to our cottage, with Kleida in our wake. I cannot be sure if Xanthippe is angrier with me or with Heraclius.

When we arrive home several village women are undressing Demetria's corpse. "She is with Pluton," one of them explains to us, "in the underworld. We will need two coins for her eyes, for her burial."

"Get away from her!" Xanthippe growls at them. "We will perform *prosthesis*—wash and dress her according to tradition. We will notify you when she is ready."

"Yes, my lady Pythia," the woman replies, contrite.

"In the meantime find some men to dig a grave!" she continues shrilly. "But first find Aegeus at the *stadion* and ask him to come here. I must consult with him."

They bow and leave.

"How do you know Aegeus? From Heraclius?" My mind is in a muddle. Too much has happened already and I cannot gain clarity.

My mother, on the other hand, seems perfectly lucid while ignoring my questions. "Kleida?"

"Yes, reverend Pythia," she addresses Xanthippe formally.

"Get cloths and a container of clean water. We will wash my mother and then dress her. She needs to be buried soon, as the summer heat is upon us."

"I will fetch Portia first."

"That is a good idea," my mother agrees tersely. "Selene, go to your chamber now. I will call you when we are ready," she dismisses me.

"I would like to help with grandmama."

"No. Do as I say."

"Yes, mother." I irately set off to my room and plop down upon my hard mattress. Demetria is no longer present to act as go-between. Years of resentment well up, coupled with today's incident. Then once again I hear Apollo's voice.

"The message, Selene. She must know the message."

"Yes, I will tell her when Aegeus arrives." I am opposed to facing my mother at this moment.

"That is a good plan," and the god relents, giving me leave to sort through the shocking details of the day.

Does Heraclius love her? Does she love him? How could that be? How has this tragedy come to pass? My world has been turned upside down. One person I love has left me in death. The second has betrayed me with my own mother. The third has never been caring of me from the beginning of my life. I started this day as a girl but have become a woman within a small movement on a sundial—a hostile woman at that.

Rage as I have never known before rips through me, devouring my soul. I want to tear the precious scrolls in my possession into shreds.

Burn the *peplos* that Heraclius' fingers had sullied with his lies. I recall Aeschylus' story of Prometheus, who Zeus chained to a rock, and whose liver was daily eaten by an eagle. Oh, Zeus, let the deceitful liver of Heraclius be ripped asunder by eagles' ferocious talons and beaks! Make him suffer!

Who is left to believe in? To trust? I am beyond sorrow to even cry. All I want to do is destroy.

I rush out of my room, past Demetria's dead body and my equally unfeeling mother, outside to the paved Sacred Way, scurrying past numerous statues of lifeless men, treasuries filled with legendary gold. A useless metal. Hard. Cold. Loveless. I recall reading in a scroll about King Midas and his golden touch. So greedy was he that he turned his own daughter into an inert metallic statue.

I want to obliterate Delphi. The Temple is a lie. Rich men paying for messages from a god. Communications that a pilgrim can interpret in his own particular, haughty, self-centered way. The Spartans have done the same recently through Xanthippe, our so-called Delphic Oracle, giving Spartan warriors a moral, righteous, even god-given excuse to wage war against Athens, the city of Heraclius. Regardless of the truth. But … is there one single truth that is superior to all others? How does one discern that truth?

I stop my headlong escape. Where am I going? To my cave, of course. My sanctuary. The one place in this desolate pitiless temple where I belong. Where I am safe.

I am already exhausted, sweat pouring down my face and chest, as I near the place where the paving ends and the gravelly road begins. Stop to breathe. Allow my aching body and emotions to calm. Because of the direction of the wind, the shouting from the *stadion* is thunderous even at this distance. Is Heraclius winning whatever event he is entered into? He would participate naked, as is the custom. I can imagine his unadorned body, shimmering with oil.

I plunge ahead, pushing myself. The exertion helps the ache and drowns my thoughts.

Finally I arrive at the cave's entrance. The inside is unwelcoming. I haven't been here in a while. The partly-shredded cushion is on the floor. I pick it up and place it gently on the couch-stone and sit upon it. Memories course through me. Memories of him. I blubber, trying to dispel the agony. Until I can cry no more and am spent. A worn-out rag of emotion.

Faintly at first, then more loudly, I hear Apollo. "You must tell them," the god insists. "Go back to your house. Explain."

Oh, will the god never leave me alone? "I don't want to be your messenger. I cannot do what you ask of me. I don't want to have your gift. It is heavy, too demanding."

I hear scraping near the entrance to the cave. Immediately I am on the alert. Is it the animal? I jump off the stone, ready to run for my life.

What I hear is not a creature. It is a man familiar to me.

"Selene," Heraclius mumbles somberly as he slowly walks into my cave.

"You! You betrayed me! You miserable hulking piece of despicable flesh! Go away!" I pummel his broad chest with my bare hands.

He twirls me around and holds my crossed arms tight with his hands against my breasts, in a wrestling maneuver. I stomp. I yell. Yet he holds me until I can calm down.

"Selene," he croons. "Selene, I love you."

"Liar!" I scream.

"It's true. I do," he insists.

"But my mother of all people…"

"It is nothing, Selene."

"How can it be nothing?"

"Through Aegeus I met Xanthippe a few years ago. I was a stupid boy, struggling with my manhood." He blushes. "She…she and I met at various times, hidden from view. She assuaged my carnal desires while I brought pleasure to her in this isolated place."

"No!! Stop!!"

"She is an older woman. As Aegeus is an older man. They taught me. Sponsored me. They are my lovers but I cannot marry either of them. I can marry you, however." He hesitates, then continues. "Selene. You have read of an *erastes*?"

"Yes," I bitingly reply. "It is an older man who is lovers with a young man. Do you mean Aegeus?"

"That is correct. I am his *eromenos*."

"The younger man of the two lovers!"

"Now you are beginning to understand."

"I understand nothing," I sputter indignantly through clenched teeth.

"Listen to me. Aegeus paid for my education. For my extensive athletic training and to participate in the Delphic Games and the Olympiad as well. I am in debt to him. Without him I could never have enjoyed all of this, which is very costly. I live with him in his villa. He introduces me to many influential Athenians in his famous *andron*, where we discuss philosophy and drink wine. My parents are poor citizens of Athens, but Aegeus is wealthy. Generous. And kind as well. He is an *agathos*—strong, brave, and rich. I am a most fortunate man to be his *eromenos*."

"What are you saying? Are you mad? Have you been running in the hot sun too long?"

"Please relax, Selene," he purrs. "You have read much of what I'm talking about. In your studies. Aegeus tells me he brings many scrolls for you to study."

"That... is just literature," I spit out. "Meaningless words on a papyrus."

"The words are real. The writing is from life. Many famous people..."

"I give up," I cannot fight any longer and my body slumps. "I cannot listen…"

He relaxes his grip on my arms. "Let me explain," he urges, calming and kind. He cautiously lets go of my arms while I practically fall to the ground. He catches me, pulls me to the couch-stone where we sit side by side on the cushion.

I am still defiant, and refuse to hold his hand although my anger is grudgingly subsiding in his company. "My mother…"

"Xanthippe is a wonderful woman."

I put my hands over my ears, unwilling to listen to her praise.

"She is a renowned Oracle," he continues. "Aegeus has come to Delphi for years, to get messages from her for his business. For Athens. Even for me. The messages she passed on helped him amass a great fortune and for me to become an accomplished, renowned athlete. He met Xanthippe but only as an Oracle. Never in any intimate way."

"Hmmmm."

"Come now, Selene. Be the civilized woman you have been educated to become. Not a sullen child." He looks at me imploringly.

"All right," I grumpily assent.

He continues thoughtfully. "Aegeus knew that Xanthippe was unhappy living in the little white house with you and your grandmother. She wanted so much more. But she could never have more. Whereas you could. With your mother's permission and his assistance, you were educated."

"She did that?"

"Yes, and more besides. She knew you had the second sight. She encouraged that gift by keeping you away from ordinary people, in sacred seclusion."

"The villagers?"

"And pilgrims, too. Your mother thought you could become the most famous Oracle ever known. Though it would take years of hard work and discipline."

As Apollo's sun suddenly comes out from behind a cloud, so my new awareness grew a moment at a time. "My mother...."

"Your mother."

"Have I misjudged her, Heraclius?"

"I thought you might say that, knowing what you know now," he continues compassionately.

"What about Aegeus?"

"An *erastes* must never have wanton sex with an *eromenos*. Aegeus could only put his penis between my thighs for release, as I did with him. Nothing more. Anything else is for barbarians."

"Is that the truth?"

"Yes, it is. Some time ago Xanthippe told me she lived in the alabaster house with her mother and a daughter. I was curious and wanted to meet the daughter. One day I went to find you. The rest of the story you know."

"What is the rest of the story?"

"That I fell in love with the daughter. You, Selene. I fell in love with you."

"Why did you lie and make up stories?"

"I have been afraid and uncertain. You are in training to be an exalted Oracle. I am nothing but an athlete playing at war games. Unworthy of you."

"You are more than that to me," I sigh.

"I know. But yet we still cannot be together. It is forbidden."

"We were together," I remind him.

"That was my arrogance. I thought I could make a difference. Change the rules. As I often alter the rules in the Games, even cheat, in order to win."

"Did Xanthippe, my mother, ever tell you about my dreams and desires?"

"No. What are those?"

"That I longed to be an ordinary woman. Not an Oracle. To have a husband and child and live a simple life far away from here."

"She never told me." Heraclius looks wistfully at me.

"Heraclius, I do not want to be a Pythia. Mother was angry with me and wouldn't allow me my desires."

"I am sorry to hear that, Selene. But she had her reasons."

"Perhaps. Did you tell her about us?"

"No. She only discovered that fact today."

"Oh, dear. Apollo and all the gods and goddesses, forgive us! No wonder she is furious."

"We are in a terrible muddle." He holds me to him and I melt into him in response. "What are we to do now?"

"Apollo's messages are my feelings," I tell him philosophically.

"What does that mean?"

I suddenly sit up. "Oh! The message. From Apollo."

"What message?"

"A great battle is coming. I was supposed to tell Demetria but she died before I could do so. And then the uproar. Where is Aegeus now?"

"Perhaps at your white house."

"Let us go find him, so I can tell him."

"Is it significant to tell him at this moment, Selene?"

"Yes, extremely important."

He helps me to my feet, but bends over and kisses me passionately on my lips. "My darling. Let us stay a little longer," he speaks amorously while caressing my breasts.

"Yes, a little longer." I embrace him, while desire envelops our young bodies. I cannot refuse him nor my craving. We undress and make love as we did before. Apollo and his message will have to wait.

After we exhaust our hunger for each other, we dress and hurry down the mountain to find Aegeus and Xanthippe.

Chapter 8

Sybota   Age 18   432 BC

Heraclius and I find the older man at the white-washed stucco house. Aegeus is speaking with Xanthippe. Hastily she leaves when we arrive.

I tell Aegeus the message in its entirety as I heard it from Apollo. "A battle will commence soon. The Corinthian navy is at sea. Near Sybota. They are poised to fight against Corcyra and Athens. Men will pay a high price. Their wives and children also. Cities and countries are at risk," I finish breathlessly.

"Then we must leave as soon as possible, tomorrow or the next day at the latest. I must consult with the Commander here at Delphi, to see what steps we must take and to gather provisions." Aegeus turns to Heraclius. "That means you as well, Heraclius. The Olympiad will be cancelled, thus there is no reason for you to continue training. The private games being held here will cease as well. Spectators will be advised to make plans to return home. Our trek to Athens will necessitate avoiding the enemy, traveling through treacherous mountain passes, as the Megara plain is still dangerously full of Peloponnesian troops."

Heraclius responds glumly. "I understand, Aegeus. I will make ready."

My mouth flies open in horror. I turn to my lover and grab his hand. "What about us?"

"There is no us in war, Selene," he answers dolefully. "We will stay long enough for your grandmother's funeral and then we must be gone."

My beloved grandmother Demetria is buried in two days with ceremony and dignity, as befitting a sacred Oracle of Delphi. The solemn procession, *ekphora*, to her burial place is attended by influential people from the private games, along with Heraclius, Aegeus, my mother and I, as well as Kleida and Portia. We bury the loom's spindle in her grave along with her favorite veil, while we place flowers around her. Kleida prepares the ceremonial meal, *perideipnon*, which all attend. I take some of the food from the *perideipnon* as an offering, leaving it at her burial place.

* * *

Demetria's absence is hard for me to comprehend. When I walk into the *gyneceum*, expecting to see her at the loom, my chest tightens with emotion. Although I attended her funeral and saw her body buried in the rock-strewn ground, her death is unreal. I expect her to re-enter the house at any moment. Her demise, coupled with the unexpected revelation of the relationship between Heraclius and Xanthippe, torments me.

My mother Xanthippe and I continue to be distant, although we were never affectionate even in the best of circumstances. The image of my mother in the embrace of Heraclius never leaves me but continues to haunt my thoughts. She is now the lone Oracle, except during her moon times, when pilgrims postpone their sessions for a few days.

Before Heraclius leaves, we steal precious hours to meet in my cave to spend time together and make love, using his bedroll for comfort. Fortunately the weather is warm. When I walk next to him, climbing the hill, holding his hand tightly in mine, I thrill to his touch. The feel of his masculinity is full-bodied while my blood thumps wildly through my veins. My breath catches in my throat as I gaze at him. He has a dimple in his chin, a mark of Aphrodite so they say. Black hair, long eyelashes, and eyebrows arching thickly over his green eyes. His hair is curly, cut short around his face, but longer at the back and coils bewitchingly at the nape of his neck. I love twining his hair around my finger and playing with it. He laughs when I do so, amused at my entertaining myself as though he is my toy.

Within a short while, we become fully acquainted with each other's bodies. When we are naked, kissing and touching, I moan from the intensity of my feelings. My life has progressed from utter isolation to almost unbearable passion. Holding me in his arms, his hairless chest rubbing against my breasts, his thighs against my groin, is a sensation I can evoke even when we are separate.

When we part for the night, I undergo the agony of farewell.

Aegeus is anxious to warn Athens and pressures Heraclius incessantly for departure, until the dreaded leave-taking arrives. Heraclius and I meet him at the Delphi camping place outside the village, where *hoplites*, spectators, pilgrims and bystanders mill around in confusion and dread.

Xanthippe is there with Kleida. My mother avoids looking at Heraclius and me. The two women bid Aegeus a quick adieu and return to Kleida's house.

I cannot let go of Heraclius' hand and cling tightly to him.

"Please, Selene," he begs me. "I must go. But I will return," he promises. "Apollo will protect you while I am gone."

With a wan smile, I force myself to be brave. "I am losing too much."

"I understand sweet one. Demetria is with you in spirit, I'm sure."

I fling myself into his arms and we embrace. "I love you, Heraclius," I murmur quietly.

"I love you, too," he replies, hugs me then climbs on his horse, which is prancing with impatience.

With much clattering of armor and equipment, neighing of horses, and shouts of civilians, the enormous group canters towards Athens. As they travel past the pair of cliffs called Phaedriades, dust follows them like a white specter as they ride through the valley of Phocis south towards Athens.

* * *

Two weeks later we are informed that a sea battle did take place at Sybota, as Apollo predicted. A disastrous battle, while many died on both sides. Neither Sparta nor Athens wants a costly war to commence and so an uneasy cease-fire is struck between them.

While waiting for Heraclius to return, I replay his words. Memories of love-making solaces as well as distresses me. Although I am willing to acknowledge details, how can I resolve his intimacy with Xanthippe and Aegeus? Healing will occur sooner or later. Time is like water dripping on a rock, suspending the particles that hold it together.

* * *

In the autumn the weather around Delphi is more unstable than usual. Far more rain and snow falls than ever before and temperatures often plunge to freezing. I impatiently wait for good weather so I can go to my cave.

My mother wants me to begin my career as Oracle, the newest Pythia of Delphi, especially with Demetria now in the ground. Although my mother and I argue at length, I refuse to proceed to the grotto and breathe the toxic fumes.

"Selene, you have the talent to be the greatest Oracle ever known," she berates me.

"I am unwilling to become an Oracle. I already hear Apollo clearly and don't want anything to interfere with that ability, regardless of the fame associated with being an Oracle."

"I don't understand why you wait for a mere mortal with dubious physical attributes to return. If indeed he ever returns," she scoffs.

Her words offend me. "He will return," I retort. "You will see, mother. Just because he left you doesn't mean he will abandon me."

With that comment Xanthippe becomes infuriated and slaps me across my face, leaving a bright red welt. "You are nothing but a whore!" and she strides out of our house.

We talk little after that day, as we each go our separate ways, me to my cave when I can, she to wherever she goes, returning only to sleep and sometimes for meals eaten in hostile silence.

* * *

Late spring. Rumor spreads throughout the village that Apollo talks to me without the necessity of my sitting in the sacred *Adyton*.

The first resident to consult with me is a local girl who comes to my white house. The young woman knocks on the wooden door frame and I answer.

"Good day, Lady. I am told you talk to Apollo. Are you able to ask Apollo questions on my behalf?" she asks frankly, standing in the open doorway.

"I would be willing to try," I declare.

"My name is Eirene. I live in the village with my husband, Mydon."

"I am glad to make your acquaintance, Eirene. I am…"

She interrupts. "Everyone knows who you are. You are Selene."

I smile affably. I pull up two little stools in the *oikos* for us to sit on. "Please be seated."

She sits cautiously and looks around. "You have a fine home," she remarks shyly.

"It was built especially for my mother and grandmother," I respond.

She rubs her arm nervously, perhaps doubting her decision to seek me out.

"How old are you?" I ask gently.

"I'm thirteen," she replies.

Although her pregnancy is showing, I detect two babies growing inside her. "You are expecting?"

"Yes," she admits self-consciously.

"Is it your first?"

"Yes."

"Would you care for some water, Eirene? Or something to eat?"

"Oh, no thank you, Lady. I cannot stay. I have work I must do."

"All right then. Tell me what you want me to ask Apollo."

"It is about my child. The midwife tells me she is worried."

"I generally talk to Apollo in my cave on the hillside. That way I am not interrupted. It is also a sacred place where Apollo can easily make his thoughts known to me. Can you attempt the steep climb in your condition?"

"Oh, yes," she answers beatifically. "May we do so after I have fed the animals and my husband early tomorrow morning? Would that be agreeable to you?"

"It would be my pleasure, Eirene." We finalize our arrangement and she hurries out the door.

The next morning Eirene arrives and follows me up the slope.

I keep my pace slow so that she can follow with comfort. From her gait and posture as well as my uneasy feelings, I can tell that her pregnancy is not going well. I worry with every step we take. This is also the first time I will consult the god about an individual. I'm apprehensive that I will not be able to hear clearly for her.

About half way up the mountain, the girl lets out a squeal, holding her belly, and stops unexpectedly. "I cannot go any further, Selene."

"The cave is far and you are too heavy for me to carry you."

"What shall we do?" Eirene asks anxiously.

"Do you think you can walk back down?" I question.

"I don't think so," she answers. "Pain is coming." With that she exclaims "Oh!" and bites her lip in order to stifle a scream. Blood is streaming down her legs.

I make an impulsive decision. "I will run down and get someone to climb back up with me."

"Hurry," Eirene moans. She describes her small house and discloses that her husband Mydon will be there.

"Here is a flat rock you can sit on," I tell her. In that moment I understand that Eirene and I have made a horrible mistake by going to the cave. I run as fast as I can to her tiny house, bringing Mydon back with me.

When her husband and I arrive, Eirene is lying lifeless on the ground. Blood has gushed from her in a huge puddle where black flies are hungrily drinking. She doesn't move or make a sound. Mydon cries out in distress, but we are too late for her. Two tiny lumps that flowed out between her thighs are dead as well along with the ruptured liver-colored afterbirth.

"I'm sorry," I cry out. "I'm so sorry. Please forgive me."

"It is not your fault," he responds dolefully. "The midwife told Eirene there could be grave difficulties." He sits in shock on the dusty ground, holding his young wife's limp hand. "I think that is why she wanted to talk to you."

I kneel down next the two of them. "Who is the midwife? I'd like to speak with her," I say gently, touching his shoulder.

"Xanthippe," he reacts huskily, his voice barely audible.

"My mother!"

She is doing the work that she wants. No wonder she goads me into taking the job of Pythia, so that she can do what she wishes instead. So she is free to be a midwife. Delphi has trapped both of us. I wonder what else Apollo demands of us. Why did I not know in advance about Eirene?

"Some consequences are destined. Fated by the gods," Apollo whispers to me, "and cannot be changed. You may hear me, feel me, and have visions, but you are not invincible. No person is sovereign. Life's plans cannot be altered by whim or wishes but are written in the stars."

How I wish I could change Eirene's outcome and her babies' as well. In *The Suppliant Women* Euripides penned a question: How to avoid one's fate by having an additional chance at life.

"Why aren't poor mortals ever allowed this,
to run life's course again, its youth and age?
As in our home, if something goes awry
we have a second chance, can rectify it."

Unexpectedly Xanthippe shows up on the path and examines Eirene's body. She gently removes the two tiny lifeless fetuses from between Eirene's legs, floating in the crimson lake, each no longer than her index finger, onto a white cloth, folds up the edges, and carries the small bloody bundle back to Delphi village, to be buried with Eirene. For the first time since I've known her, my mother weeps.

When several men arrive from the village with the donkey and a travois to help transport Eirene's dead body back to Mydon's house, I stand aside. Mydon numbly shuffles along behind the men, heading down the path, unable to believe his bad fortune.

I grieve for the dead girl as if she is my own dear sister. Although I am forgiven by her husband, I cannot easily forgive myself nor forget.

Her simple funeral brings anguish and sorrow for all of us—me, Mydon, Xanthippe, and the villagers.

The skill from Apollo can be a gift but in the future I need to remember to be humble in the presence of prophecy, or else be accursed and guilt-ridden. Apollo's bequest is not entertainment. People are not pieces of marble to be moved around as if on a game board. Human beings have lives and feelings and loved ones. I must remember I am not Apollo, but only speak on his behalf, in his name. To be as exacting as possible in my frail mortality and speech.

After that, I spend many hours counseling villagers in my sacred cave, painstaking in my words and responses. First determining that the pilgrim is able to make the steep climb with me.

My notoriety spreads beyond Delphi. Sometimes as many as a dozen people are lined up along the rocky path to my cave in hot sun or cold weather to consult with me. People too poor or without status to see the Pythia seek me out. Women who are not allowed to consult the Delphic Oracle are delighted to talk with me. No priestly hexagrams need to be unraveled. No one has to decipher obscure messages, as I endeavor to be candid and clear.

Pilgrims donate whatever offerings they can afford. I am grateful to them, their kindness and generosity, their willingness to trek on foot sometimes for days through difficult mountainous terrain to find me. I treat each pilgrim equally with honor and respect. Whatever my message is worth to them, whatever they can afford, and whatever they can give me is my motto. Each visit is a precious gift, while I grow in humility.

I am most at peace in my stony cave. The white house is yet too full of Demetria's presence as well as the palpable antagonism between my mother and me. Eventually I ask a village man to carry my wooden frame and mattress up the steep incline so that I can sleep in my cave. Bit by bit I move my belongings there and it becomes my home during warm weather.

Meanwhile I wait impatiently for Heraclius to return.

Chapter 9

THE FIRST YEAR OF THE WAR   AGE 19   431 BC

The thirty years peace treaty is broken by a surprise attack by Boeotia, an ally of Sparta, on Plataea, as predicted by Apollo. Now there is open conflict.

* * *

I receive so many combat messages from Apollo I have to stop all communications with pilgrims. I ask the village Elders to send an armed envoy, to communicate with Aegeus as well as Timon, High Official of Athens, of attacks and counter-attacks, then pass the communiques on to Pericles. They are therefore forewarned but as Apollo has explained to me, information does not necessarily dictate the outcome.

The weather has turned cold and snowy. I leave my cave and return to the warmth of the white stucco house and wait for further news, while I sleep in Demetria's old bed. I make roaring fires to warm myself while Kleida or sometimes her eldest daughter brings me home-cooked food.

I seldom see Xanthippe and have no idea where she is staying. The Delphic Oracle is shut down since no one is inclined to travel during wartime.

Hundreds of *hoplite* soldiers arrive in Delphi. The soldiers set up tents and start cooking fires on the cold, hard ground. Aegeus and Heraclius show up at my doorway, shivering in the freezing wind.

I invite them both in and close the door against the elements.

Aegeus bows. "Lady Selene, it is good to see you again. I honor your messages. We have fought and won many crusades due to your guidance. I am certain your mother is proud of you."

"Thank you for your kind words, Sir. Come in." I invite the two men inside. "Would you care for some refreshment after your long journey? Be seated. It is warm in here and you must be chilled. I can brew some lemon balm tea."

"Thank you but I cannot stay at this moment. We have brought food to Delphi since we believe there may be shortages. Many skirmishes and battles are taking place everywhere in Attica and nowhere is safe." Aegeus seems preoccupied with worry.

"I am grateful to you as always, Aegeus."

"I will oversee the unloading now," and he leaves brusquely, pulling his floor-length *himation* around himself for warmth. Snow gusts in through the open door, which I close quickly.

I am gladdened by Heraclius' appearance but alarmed at his wearing of a panoply of Athenian armor consisting of a breastplate, armor attached to his linen *chiton* at the shoulders, leg armor, a Corinthian helmet with a horsehair plume on top, dagger tucked in his waistband, and carrying a lance. He is wearing a warm red *himation*, as befitting a soldier.

"Oh, Heraclius, why are you wearing this?" I look up at his handsome face. He seems more mature than I have yet seen him.

"Aegeus purchased the panoply for me so that I may go to battle as a proper warrior," he tells me. "The lightly armed *Peltast* soldiers do not have a fighting chance in warfare."

"My dearest Heraclius. You frighten me. Why must you wage war?"

"We are in conflict with Sparta now. All able-bodied men are expected to go to battle," he asserts. "Otherwise they disgrace themselves, their families, and their city."

"But why go to combat at all?" I ask morosely.

"I find it exciting to be a man and a warrior. An honor and a privilege. Only barbarians, cowards, and women run away." His face shines with pride. "When the Spartans hear that Heraclius of Athens is coming, they will scurry from the field of battle in alarm." He grins. "I and the other men are well-trained, Selene, so there is no need to worry. We know how to fight grouped in a phalanx, shoulder to shoulder, shield to shield."

I quote a song to him from Euripides, befitting the moment:

"And why, oh why do heroes try
to prove their excellence in war?
As if a spear could guard a man
from the onslaught of life's pain."

Heraclius has no comment for me. He is immune to my love in his craving for manly action, courage, and daring.

"Oh my darling one," as I lean against him, starved for his affection and looking forward to mingling his skin with mine. I meet only a breastplate of cold bronze touching my face, which makes me shudder. "I wish you were bare-chested."

He places his arms around me and hugs me close, my head barely reaching his shoulders.

I am suddenly awake and extraordinarily alive in his presence. "It is getting dark. Do you have time? We can lie together in a real bed for once."

"I have time for you, Selene," he murmurs tenderly. "I'm sure Aegeus has everything under control."

"I don't know where Xanthippe is staying or if she will be returning home any time soon. We are alone for the moment."

We walk together into Demetria's chamber and I help him remove his helmet, his armor, leggings, and *chiton*, while I slip out of my *peplos*.

I pull my grandmother's familiar quilt over us and we are lost in the throes of love, even falling asleep for a while after lovemaking, a rare luxury for us. The white house fondly cradles us.

When he awakens, Heraclius stretches his long arms and wraps them tightly around me. He breathes into my ear. "I have an idea, my love," he speaks softly. "I have been thinking about this for a while."

"What is that, Heraclius?" I ask drowsily.

"I want you to have my child."

I sit up suddenly with a mouthful of air. "Your child?" I repeat, not sure I heard him correctly.

Yes." He pulls me onto his massive chest, while we continue our conversation. "Why not? The world has gone crazy and nothing is certain. Except that I love you and want you to carry my seed. It is the only thing of value I have to offer you."

Apollo, this is your scheme. "What have I desired all my young life?" I ask him, then answer my own question. "To have a husband, a family and a home of my own." My feelings are his messages. I sigh.

"What is it, love? What bothers you?"

"I am not sad. I'm happy. I am overwhelmed with your offer."

Heraclius laughs with joy. "Does my idea please you then?"

"Oh, yes. I am delighted!" I kiss him. "We can have a child together. It is the most romantic of ideas."

"If that is your wish."

"It is indeed my desire."

"You would have my child, even if I never return," he adds.

A cold chill passes through me. "Never return? Let us not think of that possibility," I warn him.

"Pardon my words. I am speaking thoughtlessly."

"I forgive you. But," I hesitate. "You must promise me that nothing will happen to you. That you will come back to me and our future child."

"I give you my oath," he swears. "When I return from war, we will marry. That way I will be fully accepted into Athenian society, as Aegeus suggests, as a married man."

I jump at the sound of loud knocking at my wooden front door. I pull the quilt around my nakedness and go to answer it. Aegeus stands outside, trying not to stare at my disarray.

"Is Heraclius still here?" he questions me.

"Yes, I'm sorry, Aegeus. I delayed him. I'll go get him. Please come in out of the cold night air."

He does so.

Giggling I return to Demetria's room.

Heraclius is half-dressed already. "I heard," he whispers. "I must go."

"I understand."

"Do you agree?"

"With what?" I speak softly.

"A child."

"Oh, of course. Yes, always." After he has dressed, I hand him his woolen *himation* and he strides out into the room where Aegeus waits.

"One moment," Heraclius cries to Aegeus. "I have a favor to ask of you."

"Not now. We must go. There is so much to do in a short amount of time," interrupts Aegeus.

"This is urgent."

"All right, Heraclius. What is it?"

"If I do not return from the war, do you promise to marry Selene?"

"What?" Aegeus exclaims. "Are you mad?"

"You must assure me, as my *erastes*. My beloved friend and companion." Heraclius is being his charming self. No one can refuse Heraclius when he is in that state of mind. "Please. I beg you, Aegeus."

I am eavesdropping from Demetria's bedchamber, dumbfounded, but say nothing.

"All right, Heraclius. I pledge to you I will marry Selene if you do not return."

"Swear to me on your sacred honor."

"Yes. Yes. I swear."

"Done!" announces Heraclius. "Now let us go."

I hear the door slam behind them. The pact is sealed and so is my fate.

Aegeus, Heraclius, and the *hoplites* stay for a few more days to unpack the food for the village. Then they make plans to relocate their forces to the Isthmus of Corinth, where Apollo has advised the next confrontation with Spartan troops will take place.

During those precious few days, Heraclius and I spend as much time as possible making love. I stop taking the herb *silphium* to hopefully achieve pregnancy with my beloved. Only Apollo knows whether or not Heraclius' baby will be impregnated within me, but the god isn't conferring with me on private matters. Only war dispatches are on Apollo's mind now.

At my lover's departure outside the village I am suddenly filled with dread. We have mere moments to say our goodbyes. Heraclius is looking to the future. Where am I? In an uncertain place where even Apollo can't enlighten. "Please Heraclius," I plead. "Take good care of yourself. I have grave forebodings that you will never return." I fall to my knees and cower on the ground in front of him, clutching his ankles. "I couldn't bear it."

"Get up, woman," he growls. "Look at me. Do I seem like a puny thing? An obsolete warrior? No, I am Heraclius, from Athens, and my enemies fear me. They fear even my shadow," he continues blatantly bragging.

"But Heraclius…" I weep at his feet.

"Silly woman. I will be fine. I have my spear and my companions. We will prevail. After all, the war can't last very long and I'll come home to you. And the babe," he says with utmost certainty. "Then we will marry and live in Athens."

I stand, clinging to him desperately. "No, Heraclius. Don't go. Please stay with me."

"Be well, my love," he declares, dismissing my fears. He hugs me tightly, kisses me, and leaves with the other *hoplites*.

* * *

In his absence my romantic trance grows. The song I sing is Heraclius. He is in my bones. His flesh is my flesh. Apollo put us together. Nothing can break us apart. And now with good fortune his child is growing within my body. Part of the two of us, yet unique and individual. Half of him and half of me. This is my buoyant certainty. Among all the lovers in the world, we are special. We are cherished by the god. We are fiercely protected as no one else.

As I notice my thoughts, I wonder. Have I lost my mind? Do all lovers go insane with their ardor? I sit in the little white house, listening to the spring rain pattering on the roof, re-reading a scroll written by Archilochos the poet:

"Such was my passion for love
That it twisted itself beneath my heart
And spread thick mist across my eyes,
Stealing my tender wits away."

Much time will elapse before I get a new scroll to read and study. Such is the outcome of war, when love, philosophy, and the arts dwindle and sometimes perish.

Heraclius. May Apollo protect you and bring you home soon.

Chapter 10

TYDEUS AGE 20 430 BC

"Which is best? Some say it's a host on horseback,
some say, no, foot soldiers, the wide world over;
others naval forces. To me, the best thing's
what your heart longs for."
Sappho

Thank you, Sappho. As usual you represent my thoughts and feelings.
You understand me. The best thing I long for is Heraclius.

The tempo of life runs monotonously, as spring rains will soon turn
to summer heat, followed by autumn as the earth prepares for winter
sleep.

I hear nothing. No messages from Apollo except for interminable
combat broadcasts, which I pass on to several of the village elders. Battles
rage endlessly. Blood spills like oceans of lost hope. On sea and land and
horseback, as Sappho described it. Her words comfort me, while other
writings like this one from Euripides only intensify my anxiety:

The Trojan Women:

"These are the things the Greeks have won.
These are the prizes of conquering men.
Men who win wars win nothing."

I do not understand war. What can be gained, while so much is lost?

The passage of time is dark and dank with fear and loneliness. Perhaps I will become an eternal recluse, passing on messages from Apollo, and studying the writing of Greeks. Where is Heraclius? Why does he not send word to relieve my fretful mind?

* * *

Then the day comes when my bleeding does not begin as expected. For more days afterwards. Until I have certitude. I am carrying Heraclius' child.

For women the measure of their lives is both in bleeding—and not bleeding. The rise and fall of empires is not as important as women's blood. The girl Eirene's life and death was connected to her blood. I am linked to Heraclius by my absence of bleeding, which is our child.

Why are we women considered unimportant? We are the most essential creatures on earth. Without us there is no future. No history. No empires. Only a whimper as the moon decays and declines into obscurity. Why do so many male writers revile women? I can make no sense of it. Unless men are somehow afraid of us.

Minoan men had no such fear. They were proud of their women, gloried in them, their voluptuous bodies and beauty. They made art of their women for all to see and worship.

What happened in the intervening centuries to change that parity? To turn women into slaves? To discredit their minds and bodies as if they are nothing but pigs and goats? For men to treat women as they wish with impunity?

Is that what war does? To destroy the beautiful, the home, the peaceful, because men can and seemingly want to do so? Does destruction feel better in men's loins than creation? Where is glory and honor in sudden, awful death?

* * *

I calculate the child will be born in September, during the heat of late summer. I watch my body change and swell. My breasts grow larger; the first time I remember mimicking my mother's curvaceous body. I am small and slight like my grandmother Demetria, so the change is remarkable.

Four months later I feel the wondrous quickening of life inside me. The feeling at first is slight, as if I have indigestion. Yet it continues to get stronger until I can feel specific movement inside. Later in my pregnancy I will observe the rippling of my belly as the child turns over inside me, growing ever more constricted as it matures.

Shall I contact Xanthippe, my mother? The midwife of the village. I could put myself in her skillful hands, yet I am afraid. We have had too many disputes and difficulties in our lives together.

Kleida solves the problem for me and sends for the midwife.

Xanthippe comes to the white house and enters. "Selene," she calls to me.

"I am here mother," I beckon. "I am lying down."

She comes into the room that belonged to Demetria, her mother. She looks robust and sturdy like a rock on the path to my cave. She begins without introduction. "Kleida thought you might want my help."

"Kleida is kind. Yes, I would like your help," I say agreeably.

"Very well," Xanthippe the midwife answers. "Please undress and I will examine you. I will not hurt you, but you might feel embarrassed."

I undress and lay down again.

"Put the bottoms of your feet on the mattress. Then spread your legs open," she directs me, "and relax." She spends the next few minutes with her probing fingers inside my vagina, then studying the rest of my body as well. She says nothing but focuses her attention on the patient in front of her. Her daughter's body. She looks into my mouth, has me stick out my tongue. Gazes into each eye. Feels my breasts. "How long have you been pregnant?" she asks.

"Since December last."

"Do you know who the father is?"

"Why do you need to know that?"

"Because the father's characteristics may influence the birth and health of your baby and you."

"Oh," I reply. She has knowledge I am unfamiliar with.

"Is it Heraclius?" she asks with concern.

I hesitate. "Yes, mother. It is his child I am carrying."

"He is very tall while you are petite with small bones. The baby may be large, too large for you. I will tend to you prudently."

I nod in understanding.

"I will come back in a month's time. In the meantime I want you to avoid exerting yourself. Stay away from the cave because it is a hard climb. Remain here in this house for the duration. Take daily walks through the village instead. Sit in the sunshine but do not allow yourself to become overheated."

I remember Eirene and her deadly miscarriage. Would the young woman be alive today if she had respected Xanthippe's orders? "I will do as you say."

Xanthippe grins momentarily. "I enjoy hearing you say that. You have been a willful girl with a mind of your own."

"I come by it naturally," I rejoin with grim humor of my own.

"Ha! You are right about that. We are an obstinate family, aren't we?" She pats my hand. "I will take care of you, Selene. I want the best for you and my grandchild. The baby's father would wish that as well." A shadow crosses her face and she scowls.

What does she feel about Heraclius? Did their relationship progress beyond mere physical pleasure? Is she jealous because I carry his child?

"Rest well. I will send Kleida's daughter with special food for you every day. You must be strong and healthy. This baby is what you have wanted for years, Selene. I will use all the healing arts at my disposal to make sure all goes well. I will also prepare herbs for you to take."

"Thank you, mother."

"It is my privilege, Selene." She is gone and I am left in wonderment.

When do people change without one's knowledge? Does a baby make a difference in a relationship? Even a relationship with a lifetime of squabbles and calamities? I thank Apollo wordlessly. My feelings are his messages.

I am an obedient patient. Whatever the midwife, my mother, tells me to do, I obey. I eat special foods. Take the herbal concoctions. Sit in the sunshine and amble through the village. I become a cherished member of the community. Because of the many pilgrims that I have counseled and my pregnancy, the people welcome me and are amiable. I return their affection with gratitude.

Everything changes.

* * *

During the last month of pregnancy I bleed a bit every day. Xanthippe tends me and has new potions for me to take. I can tell by her expression that she is worried, but she says nothing. I am now confined to bed. Fortunately I have scrolls to keep me company. Women from the town take turns visiting me and chatting, so that I'm not lonely. I feel privileged and humble. I know they have work to do and take time out of their arduous schedules to sit with me for a spell.

When the labor pains begin, I become frightened. Fortunately I am sitting with a neighbor and she departs to find Xanthippe, who is at my side quickly. My mother has trained several women, Phoibe and Rhoda, to assist, and they arrive with her.

She gives me a brew to swallow at once. As soon as I have done so, the contractions are stronger but not as painful. She rubs my belly with saffron powder and olive oil, massaging the concoction into my skin. "This is to help induce delivery," Xanthippe advises me. Rhoda holds my hand to comfort me.

Within a miraculously short time, the baby is born. Soon the afterbirth is disgorged intact. Xanthippe announces I am sound and without problems. She advises me to stay in bed for the remainder of the day. She administers another herbal liquid. This one makes me sleepy and relaxed.

My mind wanders. I hear the sound of an infant. A boy. He is placed naked on my breast to nurse the most important part of my milk, the colostrum. I adore the feel of his skin on mine. I notice the boy has dark hair like his father.

We have a son, Heraclius.

The midwife picks up the child from my breast. She holds the tiny one over her shoulder and lovingly rubs his back to release gas. The child sleeps in her arms, almost silent, except for little gurgling noises.

"The child is healthy, Selene," the midwife tells me. "The gods have been with you this day. You are both alive and you will recover quickly. You are a strong woman."

She seems familiar, but I suddenly cannot make out who she is. The room has become misty and my mind is perplexed.

* * *

"Tydeus. Let us call him Tydeus," the woman says to me some time later.

It is now dark and I am disoriented. "Is it morning or night? "The father is supposed to name his baby. Where is the father?" I weep uncontrollably.

"Hush, Selene."

I feel oddly detached from the child. Heraclius' son. Isn't a mother supposed to be swooning over her child, in love with the babe, like a mother lion? I feel none of that. Something must be terribly wrong with me. I cannot rouse myself, nor my love.

I sleep again and have disturbing visions. Men in battle. Crash of a spear against a helmet. Blood-soaked clothing. Wandering painfully in a forest. Or am I hallucinating?

* * *

"Selene," she murmurs softly. "Wake up daughter."

"Who speaks to me?"

"Your mother. Xanthippe. You have been sleeping for nearly two days."

"Hmmm," I reply without emotion. I hear the squalling of a baby. "Who is that?" I ask irritably.

"Your child needs to feed. Sit up, Selene."

I do so clumsily.

She places the baby in my arm, pulling the *chiton* aside so he can feed. I hold him to my nipple. He searches with his tiny mouth, sucks, then cries in desolation.

"I think your milk has dried up," Xanthippe announces anxiously. She squeezes my nipples to examine me and confirms her diagnosis. "I need to get Phoibe, the wet nurse, as I did yesterday," she exclaims and rushes from our house.

I hold the tiny infant. He is crying, red in the face from frustration and hunger. Two women enter our house.   One lovingly extracts Tydeus from my arms. Within moments he is sucking contentedly at the strange woman's breast, drinking his fill.

"Selene?"

"Yes?"

"I am so sorry. This happens sometimes."

"That is all right. The child is better off without me." I feel as though I am floating in some strange cloud, overwhelmed with disagreeable emotions, without empathy.

"What are you saying?" the other woman says scornfully.

She is angry with me but I cannot help myself.

"This is your child. You must care for him."

"My child? Are you certain?"

"Yes, I'm positive."

I muse. "He is a boy and cannot have Apollo's gift," I complain, imagining that I'm in a Greek play, wearing a gold mask. "But it's not possible," I tell them both. "Women are never allowed to play any roles in plays."

The woman who cares for me mutters to the wet nurse. "Selene is not in her right mind. What shall I do?"

"It will pass," says Phoibe shrugging her shoulders in resignation. "Give her some time to adjust. I saw this happen once before, years ago before you became a midwife."

"Did I do something wrong?" asks Xanthippe, lamenting with guilt. "Could it be the herbs? Is she having a reaction to them? The herbs never have affected any other woman before now."

"I don't know. You are a good midwife. The best we have had. I'm going to take the boy home with me for now. It will be easier for everyone."

"All right. Thank you for your help, Phoibe."

"Be at peace, Xanthippe."

* * *

The next few days pass as if in a dream. I never know if I'm waking or sleeping. A bowl is shoved in my face. I recognize soup and taste it. It is peppery and I push it away impatiently.

"You must eat, Selene," I hear a voice.

"I am not hungry," I tell the voice.

"Try. You must nourish yourself."

I fall unconscious only to be overwhelmed by bewildering visions. Crowds cheer for their favorite athlete, who sprints up the path to a cave where he wrestles with a one-eyed leopard. I drift, withdrawing into a world of lunacy ruled by the goddess of the moon.

* * *

With a start, I wake completely. It is night. The wind is blowing furiously outside. I go to the front door and open it, almost blown back by the gale, and shut the door quickly. The night is the dark of the moon. I'm ravenous and go to the little kitchen.

"Selene?" Xanthippe is at my side instantly. She has been waiting for me.

"Mother," I say when I see her.

She sighs in relief. "So you recognize me at last."

"I'm hungry, Mother," I tell her.

"I'm glad," she groans. "I was so worried about you."

"You were?" I am astonished at her concern. Aren't we rivals? Doesn't she hate me? Instead I ask. "Is there something to eat?"

"Oh, yes. Let me get you something. We have yogurt. And grapes, too."

"Is there lamb?"

"No, but I will make sure Kleida cooks a chicken for you tomorrow."

"I want lamb!"

"We won't have lamb until spring," she reminds me edgily.

"Spring. When is that?" I hold the bowl of watery yogurt she offers to me and slurp it, still standing, until I am sated. "I had the strangest dreams, Mother."

"You're awake now, Selene, and I am here."

"I'm so tired."

"I will make sure to get you chicken liver tomorrow, too. Would you like a little wine? You can have a glassful of retsina if you like."

"Yes," and I gulp the pungent concoction down in one swallow. The wine warms my stomach. "I feel better now."

"Rest my daughter. You'll feel better in the morning."

"I will?" I ponder for a moment. "All right then. Good night."

"Good night, Selene."

I return to Demetria's room, and slide under the quilt, fast asleep once more.

* * *

During the next few days Xanthippe is good as her word. She feeds me chicken livers, red wine, grapes, and raw eggs mixed with yogurt. I am weak and disoriented, but can sit at the little wooden table for a few minutes to eat, then return exhausted to bed.

She murmurs. "I don't understand what has happened to you. You seemed perfectly well at the birth. But then suddenly you were not."

"The scrolls would know," I tell her. "Scrolls have many answers. Do you have medical scrolls you could study? Asclepius, the god of medicine, would know what to tell you. Or Hygieia."

"I only hear Apollo." She wrinkles her forehead, trying not to scold me. "That is a sound idea, though. When Aegeus comes here, I will ask him about scrolls."

"When is he coming again?"

"I don't know," she retorts angrily. "This horrible war! Do you still get messages from Apollo?"

"Now and then, but they don't make sense. Too much violence and death. I don't feel strong enough to focus my attention on them. The messages make me cry. Do pilgrims come to the *Adyton* for you?"

"Seldom. The war keeps most people away. There is often fighting, especially in Boeotia, which makes it impossible to travel here."

I change the subject. "How is Tydeus doing?"

"Tydeus is thriving at Phoibe's house. He grows bigger every day! Soon he will be as big as his father…" Xanthippe stops suddenly, the subject painful to both of us.

"That is good to hear. Please thank Phoibe for me." Tears well up uncontrollably in my eyes. "Where is Heraclius, mother? What is happening to him? When will he come back?"

"I am sorry, Selene. I cannot answer those questions."

"I cannot either." I leave the table and return to bed, drained by nameless fatigue, melancholia, headaches, and nightmarish moods. Insufferable loneliness is my companion.

Sappho understands my solitude. I remember some of her words for the first time since I took ill.

"The moon is down,
and the Pleiades.
It's midnight,
time passes,
and I lie alone."

Heraclius. His name is my prayer.

Chapter 11

AEGEUS   AGE 21   429 BC

Apollo continues to send war messages. The god does not choose sides, only imparts dispatches through whatever means, Seer or Oracle, at his disposal. Without maps in front of me I am unfamiliar with some names and places and cannot discern the importance of them nor the battles that ensue. I relate communications to the village Elders, desiring that they transmit those messages for generals to translate into meaning. As the Elders send envoys to Athens on behalf of Apollo, while similar missives are undoubtedly being sent to Heraclius' enemy, the Peloponnesians.

* * *

I gain strength little by little. Some days I can climb to my cave.

Tydeus celebrates his first birthday. He is a happy child, living in Phoibe's house with her children. Xanthippe visits him every day, often staying at their home. The boy is tall for his age, good looking, self-aware, and beginning to talk. He has dark hair like his father, a coppery complexion, with blue eyes like mine. I call on him whenever my mother is absent from Phoibe's house, but he seems more attached to Phoibe and her family than to me.

Where is your father, my son? He has been gone almost two years.

If Heraclius is dead, wouldn't a comrade have transported his armor to Athens for Aegeus? Returning a fallen warrior's armor to his family is the proper way to conduct combat. Does that mean Heraclius might be alive?

Often a truce can be requested to gather the dead. Has something horrendous befallen the entire company of *hoplites* so no one remained to request his body?

I think of Heraclius and his comrades in arms. Where in the desolate Spartan land, the Peloponnese, might their decomposing bodies rot in the sun? Unburied by their opponents, unconsecrated, left to putrefy above ground, prey for worms and vultures.

Euripides echoes my thoughts when he wrote *The Trojan Women*:

"Thousands of Greeks struggled and fought
bravely. Thousands of these thousands died.
For what? Those who died
will never see their children.
No wife came to prepare them
for the grave;
they lie here, all here,
in this foreign, angry earth, this earth that hates
their dead, decaying bones."

Heraclius was connected to me for four precious years, before I lost him to battle. I don't understand war or warriors. Why do men restlessly start battles or covet a bit of land that isn't theirs? What insults them into action? Is pride and revenge worth more than lives and families? Why do they take up arms against neighbors? What do they hope to gain?

Kleida's oldest daughter brings me food every day, as did her mother, sometimes clambering up the stony path to my cave to do so.

* * *

Autumn has come again. The season of harvest. Leaves have burst into scarlets, oranges, and purples, and float to the ground and soon to turn to bits, composting where they fall.

As if in answer to a supplication, Aegeus comes to Delphi soon after Tydeus' birthday. He arrives at the little white house. Xanthippe is home, unusual for her, while I study in my chamber.

She answers the door. "Aegeus," she shouts in surprise.

I am on my feet running to the door to greet him. "Aegeus. I am so glad to see you again."

"As I am honored to see both of you. Two revered messengers of Apollo."

Xanthippe invites him in. "Would you care for some watered wine? It is not very good but all we have."

"No, thank you honored lady. Let me be brief. It is Selene I wish to speak with. May we have a moment?"

"Yes, of course. I'm going to Kleida's house to spend the night, Selene, so there is no hurry."

"Very well, mother."

Xanthippe grabs her *himation* and quickly departs. Dried leaves blow in through the open door and I close it hastily.

Aegeus and I sit in the oikis, the public room, upon little unembellished stools, which can be moved from room to room.

He begins without overture. "I have not heard from Heraclius since I last saw you."

"I have not learned anything either. Nor have I received messages from Apollo about him. I know only of battles and skirmishes in distant lands."

"If Heraclius has died in battle, it is customary that his fellow *hoplites* return the armor to me."

"Yes, that is what I understand."

"I have never received anything, however, and no dispatches either. There is ample time to have done so. Perhaps there was a massacre and they all died. I am troubled that he lies unburied on unhallowed ground. There is no other explanation."

"Do you truly believe that is what transpired, Aegeus?"

"Yes, Lady Selene. I am afraid there is no alternative viewpoint."

"I cannot speak of this. If I do, emotions will soon overwhelm me."

Aegeus continues. "I am told you have borne a son of Heraclius. Tydeus."

"Yes, Tydeus. He is an amazing child."

"I can easily believe that, knowing his parentage."

"He currently lives with Phoibe, his wet nurse, and her family."

"Tydeus should be looked after as his father was cared for. To be well-educated. Brought up in prosperous circumstances. To have all the benefits that Heraclius once had. He deserves advantages as a child of an illustrious family."

"That would be a wonderful opportunity for him."

Aegeus leans close to me. "Do you know that Heraclius extracted a promise from me? To marry you if something happened to him. I never believed anything could happen as he lived a charmed life, but I swore anyway."

"Yes, I overheard your vow that night long ago."

"Selene. I want to make good on that promise."

I inhale sharply, wondering. Is this good news? Or bad?

"I wish to marry you and adopt Tydeus. To bring you both to Athens as my family. To introduce you to the best people in the city. To see you both are well cared for and cherished as Heraclius would have wanted."

"I am overwhelmed."

"You may not have heard but plague swept through Athens last year."

"Yes, I heard that terrible news."

"Even the great Pericles, orator and general of Athens, along with several members of his family, died not long ago of the sickness."

"His death is a great loss to Athens."

"That is true." He grimaces. "The Great Wall of Athens is both a blessing and a curse. We are safe from enemies. But conditions worsen inside the sealed off city, while epidemic overflows the streets, uncontrolled. Partly from rubbish and debris, partly from disease delivered by foreign ships, as well as moldering bodies of victims."

I shudder listening to the details.

"When the plague struck, I left Athens on one of my ships, while I consigned my property and business into the care of trustworthy slaves. I stayed on the island of Naxos until the danger was past. Just recently I returned to set my affairs in order. I have now freed those particular slaves for their unflinching and courageous service to me, risking their lives to remain in the city."

"You have always been generous, Aegeus."

"Generosity is its own reward," he declares. "My business is more prosperous than ever." He becomes perfectly serious. "Selene, tell me you will accept my offer. I have never married and I am not young anymore. A family is essential in Athenian society. I will also be helpful to you and Tydeus." Aegeus seems eager.

I hesitate.

"I have deliberated about this a lot, Selene. I am not being impulsive."

"You are not an impulsive man," I agree.

"I understand you may not love me as you loved Heraclius. Perhaps in time you can grow fond of me. Especially as I can be useful in your son's education and livelihood. Provide you both with a lifestyle of ease and comfort that will continue even after I am gone. I will change my will to put some of my worldly possessions into Tydeus hands, to be initiated when he has come of age. If I die before that, Timon will be his guardian, administering the estate for Tydeus until he is old enough."

"May I think about your offer, Aegeus?"

"I am only in Delphi overnight. We rushed to get here, while battles continue elsewhere. I came to talk to you and to ascertain your answer to my proposal. Autumn has arrived and we need to return before winter is upon us."

"Oh. Well in that case I happily accept for both my son and me." Who is being impulsive now?

He stands quickly. "That is wonderful news indeed. " He hugs me gently. Not as a lover but as a father figure. "Is there much for you to pack?"

"Very little, Aegeus. Mostly scrolls."

"I will purchase whatever you might need or want. There is fighting everywhere, so it may take time to reach Athens, and necessitate numerous detours."

"I am not worried about that," I respond.

"Is there something else you are worried about?" he asks hesitantly.

"I am concerned about Tydeus. He is attached to Phoibe and her family here in the village who have raised him since birth. I hope it won't be too big a shock for him to leave. Fortunately Phoibe has weaned him and he eats solid food now."

"Children are flexible and can adapt to new situations," he counters.

"I am sure you are right." But I am not at all certain. "Let us collect him in the morning after we eat something. Would you like to sleep here? There is an extra bed…"

I am uneasy and don't want him to slumber with me. That matter would be dealt with later. After we arrive in Athens.

"Xanthippe has the largest bed chamber, so you will be most comfortable there." I realize that Xanthippe had divined this situation and thus left to stay overnight with Kleida.

"I would like that. You are quite hospitable, Selene."

I swallow nervously. "Thank you, Aegeus."

"I look forward to our formal wedding in Athens. It will likely be an event unheralded in recent times."

"Yes. I look forward as well," I fib. I have no idea what the event could look like, having never attended a formal wedding.

We settle down for the night. Aegeus in Xanthippe's bed. Me in Demetria's chamber, as my own bed had been moved to the cave. He is soon snoring while I have difficulty sleeping. Am I making the right decision? Is Heraclius indeed dead? I wish I had my own personal oracle to consult, while Apollo is silent.

* * *

Early the next morning we dress, eat a little. I gather together the price-less scrolls. My favorites I will take with me. I leave the rest in the care of Kleida and Xanthippe, to be delivered to Athens or picked up at Delphi at some point in the hopefully not-too-distant future. Then Aegeus and I set off for the village, first to say goodbye to my mother, then to collect Tydeus.

Kleida is more affectionate than my mother, who acts standoffish. "I will see you again, if that is the wish of the gods," Xanthippe ex-presses coolly and embraces me tentatively.

I forgive my mother as she has had to deal with much and perhaps saved my life in childbirth as well. "Be well, mother," I respond grace-fully.

Then the four of us set off for Phoibe's home to collect my son. The child is teething, feverish, and cranky. He cries when I attempt to pick him up and will not be comforted.

"My lady," Phoibe murmurs. "Perhaps my eldest daughter Melita can travel with you, to care for the lad. He has known her his entire, tiny life, and would thus be soothed. She is only twelve but she has cared for her younger brothers and sister, as well as Tydeus. Thus, she is mature for her age."

"What a wonderful idea."

I ask Aegeus and he agrees whole-heartedly. "A baby on a long trip would mean a lot of work. Tydeus has lived with Melita and he will be more peaceful if she travels with us."

So it is agreed that Melita will trek with us to Athens, to care for the baby. The girl packs a few items for herself and Tydeus.

At the edge of Delphi village a small troop of a dozen well-armed Athenian *hoplites* with extra horses are waiting for us. They will protect us, and the scrolls on our journey. I am helped to awkwardly mount a docile mare and settle onto the blanket, holding on to the reins apprehensively. Melita is given a *Pindos* pony to ride. Aegeus sits his own horse, an exquisite grey *Andravida* stallion, while Tydeus is placed on his lap and tied to his body to keep him from falling off. We set off on our adventure, cantering slowly for the time being.

The *hoplite* contingent is divided, six in front and the rest in back, to defend us from foes, all riding sturdy horses from Thessaly.

We ride in a glorious autumn day. The light is clear and glittering off the almost-bare trees, as the orange, purple, and red leaves fall to the ground, making mounds of extravagant colors. The air is beginning to chill and rain sprinkles intermittently. We hold our cloaks tight to our bodies. The *hoplites* give each of us an extra blanket as well.

To prevent slipping, the horses pick their way carefully down the mountain slope into the valley of Phocis. At our altitude we pass evergreens, pines and cypress, then continue downhill through olive groves below, the richest such orchards in Greece. As we descend, we can see the coastal plain from the slopes. When we reach level ground, horses are whipped into a gallop as we head towards Athens. We have no time to lose, amid Spartan troops and the change of season.

I have read extensively about various locales yet seeing them with my own eyes is breathtaking. Whenever we ride through a new area, I ask Aegeus what it is called, so adding reality to the written word and maps.

The area is forested, although not as thick as it was in former days. For hundreds of years wood has been harvested for both Delphi village and sacrificial fires for the Temple. Shrubs and cypress, beech and chestnut trees surround us, fallen leaves a dull brown. Poppies had been blooming but all we see now are bare green stems as the brilliant red petals have dropped long ago. Periodically we hear an eagle or hawk, its screams distinctive, as it glides overhead, scanning for prey.

As we ride along, our legs wrapped tightly around the horses' bodies, I am in awe of the changing landscapes of Greece. Rocky outcroppings on hillocks of granite with greenery at the base. Mt. Parnassus recedes behind us, growing smaller by the day.

Within the first day I am receiving messages from Apollo. The god gives me valuable instructions on what route to take, how to avoid enemy soldiers, and to stay far away from battles and skirmishes. I am grateful for the god's help in this matter.

Commander Aindrea of the *hoplite* group rides over to Aegeus. I overhear their anxious conversation.

"We must detour around Thebes," Aindrea tells him. "We cannot risk being seized."

"Very well, Commander," Aegeus responds. "What is the best way?"

"We will need to ride southwest, towards Corinth, then east, close to Megara. As you know Peloponnesian troops can be anywhere. Megara is aligned with Sparta, as is Corinth. With luck the soldiers will have departed the area and traveled to Thebes to overwinter."

"What does Apollo say?" Aegeus asks me.

"That is the best plan," I answer after a short consultation with the god.

* * *

Fortunately Tydeus calms down on our long trip, entranced and entertained by what he sees. Melita cares for the toddler during breaks, while Aegeus and I take turns holding the child on our laps as we ride. Sometimes a *hoplite* offers to do so, which gives the boy great delight. The child revels in the stride of a horse, rocking him to and fro, sometimes at full gallop, with the wind blowing through his thick, black hair. He scrutinizes the *hoplites*, dressed in their armor, red *chlamys* draped around their shoulders, as they give orders and bellow to each other. Tydeus wants to assist in pitching our tent every night for us to sleep in. However, he is too young to be of support, so he toddles around the campground, amusing everyone with his antics. He is learning quickly and attempts new words on our journey.

* * *

Because of Apollo's assistance, we get to Athens quickly and safely.

When our group arrives at Athens, Commander Aindrea points to the famous Themistoclean Wall. "This is the defensive wall which extends all the way around the city, to the port of Piraeus, protecting the city and the harbor from invasion."

Aegeus rides within earshot of me. "We are at the entrance to the city, the Acharnian Gate, one of four gates into Athens. We will pass through the Gate after we are properly identified. Piraeus is loaded with war ships—*triremes*—as well as merchant vessels, some from as far away as Sicily, Egypt, and Ionia. My ships are at anchor there as well," he finishes proudly.

Commander Aindrea talks with the guards on duty and we are soon allowed entrance.

As we arrive into the city, I am awestruck. This is Athens I have read about in my scrolls. The city that Apollo volunteered messages for Athenian politicians, merchants and generals. Home of Heraclius and Aegeus—and many other famous men.

The glory is staggering. Even from this distance I can easily see the Parthenon on the distant Acropolis. There are no suitable words to describe the splendor. I'm in awe of the beauty and the majesty that stands high above the city below.

Aindrea gives orders. "Let us rest the horses for a while. There is a trough here for them filled with water." We dismount, while the horses eagerly drink their fill.

Tydeus is whining and struggling to be released from Melita's arms.

"The baby is hungry," Melita whispers to me, holding the baby tightly.

"I know. Here is a piece of pita bread he can chew on until we get to Aegeus' villa."

Aegeus tells me. "We will resume our travel in a few minutes, then finish the last leg of our journey. My villa is not far from here, where we will eat and rest."

As I stand and behold the impressiveness of the Acropolis, Commander Aindrea continues. "My Lady, about fifty years ago the former Parthenon was under construction when the Persians invaded and sacked Athens. The building was burned and looted, along with ancient temples and everything else on the rock. Debris was cleared from the site and buried ceremoniously in a pit on the hill, which is now a war memorial." Aindrea is obviously proud of the city that he protects. "Since then we have built the wall you see here, to defend Athens and its harbor." He strides back to his comrades.

Aegeus continues the dialogue. "Pericles was in charge of creating all the buildings on the immense outcropping there until his death a short time ago. He was strong; it took him six months to die of plague. Pericles was a remarkable man and will be grieved by all in Athens."

"I can only imagine. What splendid works he commissioned!"

"Inside the completed Parthenon is an enormous statue of the goddess Athena, patron of Athens, about five *kalamos* high, the same height as the Themistoclean Wall. I gazed upon the statue once. Poets can most likely describe the statue's splendor, but I cannot muster lyrical words."

I shake my head in amazement. "I can scarcely conceive of living in this city, with so much grandeur and loveliness. Unlike Delphi village and my cave."

"Most of my life was spent in this city. Except for a short interval when I returned from Naxos, I have been gone almost two years. I have missed Athens greatly and will be glad to be home."

Buildings and columns atop the rocky Acropolis that makes Athens famous are glowing crimson in the wintery twilight.

Aindrea shouts orders. "Mount up. We will finish our exceptional task this day. We must arrive before darkness falls."

Chapter 12

ATHENS   AGE 22   428 BC

Fourth year of the war. Fortuitously we arrived in Athens before the invasion of Attica by King Archidamus of Sparta. Without Apollo's help we would never have gotten through safely and in time. We would eventually hear from military envoys that destruction is widespread, crops have been burned, people are starving, while refugees are fleeing the countryside.

* * *

As we ride through Athens, I feel as though I am back at the Sacred Way of Delphi. Exquisite white marble buildings, temples, and statues are sited gracefully. Their impressive appearance will surely be superb by the light of day.

When we arrive at Aegeus' villa, the wealth, size, and magnificence of his opulent home overwhelms me. The front entrance is protected by a tiled roof, triangular in contrast to the perpendicular walls, held up by four graceful marble columns with Doric capitals carved on top. Pieces of cut pink marble designate a picturesque, intricate pathway to the door.

Several slaves meet us and take the horses to the stable.

"Thank you for your service," Aegeus tells the soldiers.

Aindrea responds, "It has been our honor, sir, to ensure you and your family arrived safely." The Athenian *hoplites* gallop off to their military headquarters located elsewhere in Athens, in a humble part of the city.

With pride Aegeus ushers us upstairs to the second floor and then to our rooms. Oil lamps have been lit in the halls and chambers. There are four bedrooms, each with a bed and a luxurious thick mattress. Instead of old quilts, the coverlets are made of colorful silk, filled with goose feathers, and embellished with birds, flowers, and other artful designs.

Melita has a small room of her own at one end of the hall, with a niche for the baby. His crib is made of rare wood carved with mythical figures, with drapery over the top. Obviously Aegeus assumed Tydeus and I would move to Athens.

Standing against the wall is an illuminating oil lamp on a table with two low-backed chairs facing it. A window with delicate linen curtains overlooking the dark courtyard completes the room. Melita places Tydeus in the crib and covers him. The child is worn out from our travels and falls asleep immediately. The pita bread assuaged his hunger for now.

"Oh," Melita speaks innocently. "Are we at Mt. Olympus with the gods?"

Aegeus smiles with pleasure. "Rest yourself, girl. You will be served a meal in your room presently." He leaves Melita and the baby to rest.

"Come with me, Selene, to our room," and he takes me by the hand to lead me.

"Our room?" I am pleasantly surprised by his gesture. It is the first moment we have been alone since we left Delphi, during which time he never touched me.

The L-shaped bedroom is at the middle of the hall on the second floor. A marble statue placed on a short pedestal, with a gorgeously clad female korai, graces the wall outside the door. Inside, the bed is three times larger than the one I slept in at Delphi. Silk hangings decorate the wall and are gracefully looped over the tall bed frame with an identical silk coverlet. A large window hung with filmy curtains overlooks the courtyard, which is too dark to see. A table with intricately carved legs like lions stands in the middle of the spacious room. Two high-backed chairs with similarly carved feet are placed at either end of the table. An empty red vase with figures artistically painted on it has been placed on the table along with an ornately designed oil lamp, already lit by attending slaves.

"It's too late in the season to fill the vase with flowers," he explains. "With the coming of spring this room will resemble a garden."

I spot a life-sized nude statue holding a javelin, standing near the window. "It looks like…can it be?" I exclaim in both shock and pleasure.

"Yes, it is a statue of Heraclius I commissioned before the war started. He modeled for it himself. Is it not a good likeness?"

"I almost believe he could walk over to us and speak!"

"I'm glad you are pleased." He ambles over to a small alcove covered with a gleaming white linen curtain embroidered with spring flowers. "These are all for you." He pushes aside the cloth and proudly displays a number of brand-new silk *chitons* hanging from pegs. Several himations are included, for warm weather as well as cool, along with colorful veils to drape over my head.

I examine the luxurious items of apparel. "They are beautiful! Are they for me?"

"Yes, I ordered them before I traveled to Delphi to find you. In case you said yes. I thought you would be happy to find them when you arrived."

"Oh, Aegeus!" I hug him then briefly kiss him on the lips—the first time I had ever done so. "How lovely. What a kind man you are."

He doesn't move away but enjoys the attention. "If you agree, this room will be ours to share," he whispers shyly.

"If you are trying to pamper me, you are succeeding."

"However, I think it is fitting if we wait to live together in this room until after the wedding," he mentions with consideration of the social mores of Athens. "I do not wish to insult you or sully your good name. I will sleep in an extra bedroom next to Tydeus until after our wedding."

"My good name?" I murmur. I had a child out of wedlock with a man who disappeared during wartime, presumably dead in a foreign land. I rode for hundreds of miles with a group of soldiers and a gentleman I only knew slightly. Both my mother and grandmother had children without benefit of marriage as well. I am amused and strangely touched by his chivalry. Then I realize that he is safeguarding his own reputation by acting with utmost propriety. "When will we be married?" I ask modestly.

"Soon!" as he grabs my small body by the waist and twirls me around. "You are so small. I didn't realize…"

I laugh in delight. Then he kisses me impulsively on the cheek.

Will Aegeus be a lover as well as husband? My heart begins to thaw with hopefulness. The statue near the window stands motionless. Would Heraclius be jealous if that will be the case? Accordingly I will ask Aegeus if he can move the statue elsewhere, perhaps to the hall or downstairs.

"I will show you the rest of the house tomorrow morning. After you have rested and it is light."

The slaves serve a small meal in my room and, exhausted, I fall sleep in my new, luxurious bedroom.

* * *

Aegeus shows up in the morning as promised. "Would you like to have a tour now?" he asks.

"Oh, yes. I slept well and am energized. Please show me around."

"That new *chiton* is very attractive, Selene."

I blush in gratitude. "Thank you for your thoughtfulness, Aegeus."

He hikes his yellow *himation* further onto his shoulders. Aegeus is an average man with an average physique.

Then he leads me down the stairs to a large *andron* on the first floor that we had passed through last night. "This is one of two *androns*, meeting rooms for men only, where my friends will come for entertainment and discussion. Next to that is the *oikos*, the public room for mixed gatherings. Each chamber has a doorway through to the next, so the house has many inter-linking rooms. The same is true with the second floor. Here is a door leading to the courtyard from the *oikos*."

The house is shaped in a square with four sides, two stories high, enclosing an open courtyard in the middle as high as the roof. The gable, also triangularly shaped, is paved with hundreds of red clay tiles, each one attached to the next.

The courtyard is nothing like I have ever seen before. Trees, shrubs, flowers, all combined in elegant and artistic patterns of greens and soon-to-be flowering colors. Some trees are short, others reach almost to the roof. Trees—almond, pistachio, and pear—are planted against a low southern wall. Interspersed are tall cypress and shorter junipers. Scattered among the greenery are low wooden chaise lounges with carved legs and backs, with colorful plump pillows arranged on them for utmost comfort. Next to each lounge is a table. There are enough tables and chairs to host a large party. A number of marble statues fixed on pedestals, every bit as skillfully wrought as those at Delphi, are artfully placed. The entire enclosure is one of peaceful serenity and visual enchantment.

"Athenian summer is much hotter than at Delphi so the open-air courtyard is a blessing. We will spend much of our time out here."

I sigh in contentment. "Melita is correct. We are in a home meant for gods."

He beams with pride. "It took years to construct this. I personally designed the architecture, although I hired professionals to fashion it into reality."

"Oh, Aegeus. What a glorious place to live."

He takes me by the hand, interlacing his fingers with mine, walks over to one of the lounges, reclines, and pulls me onto his lap. He is shaking with desire. His short yellow *peplos* has ridden up his leg, the evidence clearly outlined. "Selene," he begins. "Thank you for saying yes. I hope you will be as happy here as I have been." He puts his arms around my shoulders and nuzzles my neck. Then he pushes my hair aside and begins to kiss the skin underneath. His well-trimmed beard prickles.

I lean into him. "I am happy now."

Abruptly he stops himself.

"What is the matter, Aegeus?"

"We must wait for the wedding. I am a proper man." He helps me to stand. He has become red in the face, and arranges his clothing, covering himself. "The slaves..." he mentions. "We must be decorous."

"We could go to our chamber," I suggest, "and continue."

"No. We will wait."

"As you wish," I agree half-heartedly. Aegeus has willpower such as Heraclius never possessed. The athlete was impulsive and reckless. Which behavior do I prefer?'

* * *

As always, Aegeus is in charge. He hires wedding advisors to handle a myriad of details. "We must have a wedding soon!" he explains to them. No one in Athens ever heard of a wedding to be carried out in such a short time.

"Yes, Sir. We will do our best."

Invitations are sent out to illustrious, powerful, wealthy, and influential citizens of Athens. Even though it is wartime, many locals of importance attend.

Workers and slaves enter and depart the sumptuous house during the next few days. Bringing food. Flowers. Extra tables and chairs are transported into the villa. Sheep and goats are sent as gifts from various weddings guests, to be roasted and served at the wedding feast.

I am fitted with a beautiful, floor-length, red *chiton* made of shimmering silk, with a matching red veil and *chlamys*. Although commonly the groom is to appear naked at the wedding feast, Aegeus is too modest to do so, and instead is wearing a short red *chiton* that matches my own.

Guests arrive in litters and sedan chairs carried by strong slaves. The throng is wearing copious amounts of anklets, necklaces, bracelets, and headbands, all inlaid with jewels. They sparkle in the sunlight as they walk onto Aegeus' estate.

At my prompting, Aegeus has memorized a line from Alcestis written by Euripides and recites it to the gathering at the start of the festivities.

"Once with pine-torches from Mount Pelion and bridal songs I entered, holding the hand of my dear wife, and a clamorous throng followed, praising the blessedness ...we had become man and wife."

Strong and watered wine, along with delicious honey mead, is served with numerous courses of various sumptuous foods. The ostentatious banquet lasts several days, which commemorates the public celebration and recognition of Aegeus' marriage to me.

I have no dowry, but that doesn't seem to upset him. "I am wealthy enough for both of us," he jokes when I bring up the subject.

During the feast he announces, "Some of you have whispered of the lack of dowry. A dowry is of no matter in our marriage. Selene is valuable as precious gold in the eyes of the world, as Seeress, daughter and granddaughter of world-renowned and well-respected Oracles of Delphi. Her son, Tydeus, is born of the great athlete Heraclius. It is my privilege and honor to take Selene as my wife and to adopt the child as well, who is now my son. In time we will have more. She already demonstrates that she is fertile."

Aegeus then presents me with a necklace consisting of tiny gold beads with an exquisitely crafted electrum honeybee medallion hanging at my breasts. "The bee is sacred and so is my wife," he exclaims.

The guests clap heartily. Many of them are already drunk, and won't remember the speech later.

Our most famous wedding guest is Captain Teris, although now aged, who had participated in the legendary battle of Salamis.

Tydeus joins the gathering during the announcement of his adoption, while the Captain bounces the boy on his knee, regaling him with stories of battle and victory.

"At Salamis, our fleet defeated the Persians and destroyed 800 of their ships by tact and cunning," Captain Teris tells the boy, while wedding guests listen attentively. "According to Herodotus, it is believed that the naval maneuver saved undefended Athens from total destruction. The Persians were razing many buildings and had attacked the Acropolis as well. To prevent that from happening again, we built the Themistoclean Wall around Athens, as well as the Long Wall to Piraeus," he finishes pompously.

That night the men troop to the bedroom on the second floor, where they stand outside the closed door to witness my formally joining with Aegeus.

My husband is dizzy with wine and can't perform. Instead we make a demonstration of great carnal noises, grunting, crying, and thrashing around, while wedding visitors drunkenly cheer and applaud.

Several days later, guests depart and our household becomes quiet. Slaves work dutifully to clean up the disarray, to restore the villa to its former immaculate condition.

* * *

Although we have officially become united in the presence of witnesses, Aegeus and I are still virgins to each other.

"Let us go to bed, wife," he says blearily. "I have waited long enough."

We peel off our respective red *chitons*, his now stained with wine, sweat, and food. He chuckles drunkenly at the destruction of his costly, although now ruined, wedding outfit. Aegeus has consumed strong wine throughout the lengthy wedding banquet and festivities, and is still somewhat inebriated through the long celebration

He pulls me onto the mattress and climbs on top of me. He is engorged and ready for sex. But once he is inside me his erection vanishes.

"Oh, gods," he gasps. "This has never happened to me before." He tries again, but without success.

"That is all right, Aegeus," I apologize on his behalf. "We have the rest of our lives to make up for tonight."

"Hmmmp," he grunts, rolls off me onto the bed, and is soon breathing heavily.

I pull the silk coverlet, decorated with designs of birds-of-paradise, over him and sit up. I am disappointed, but resign myself to future satisfaction. I look toward the window, glad that the statue of Heraclius has been removed, and cannot be a silent bystander to frustration and humiliation.

* * *

The annoying experience wouldn't be the last time. Oddly enough Aegeus always loses his erection when attempting to make love to me. His impotence becomes such a daily experience, we each lose the desire to even attempt lovemaking. We sleep together in uneasy slumber.

"I am hoping for sons of my own," he grumbles to me one night upon retiring.

"Heraclius never experienced this problem," I mention. "I'm sorry, husband. What can I do?"

"Nothing," he retorts curtly. "But do not mention his name again!"

Reprimanded, I change the subject. "Should we consult a physician?"

"I would be the laughing stock of Athens within a few days."

"Perhaps the scrolls have some advice."

"Your ever-lasting scrolls!" he criticizes me. "Of what use are they to me now?"

His anger brings me to tears. "Perhaps Apollo..." I whimper.

"This problem is entirely your fault, Selene. If you were a better wife..." Aegeus doesn't finish the statement, but scrambles out of bed, wraps a *chlamys* around him, and leaves.

Heraclius. Why did you pledge me to a cold, heartless man? What good is your promise? I am lost in misery.

Euripides in *Trojan Women* wrote about a generation of women who lost their loves through war and were consequently married to second husbands:

> *"They say that a single night in a new man's bed softens the loathing, but*
>   *not for me.*
> *I despise the woman who gets remarried, who, in the passionate arms*
>   *of another,*
> *Forgets the love of her first man."*

From that night forward Aegeus sleeps in an extra bedroom, permanently abandoning me, as well as his hope for sons of his body.

Chapter 13

THE ANDRON   AGE 23   427 BC

Fifth year of war. Peloponnesians attack and occupy much of Attica, including Salamis and Plataea, under the command of the regent of Sparta, Cleomenes.

* * *

Aegeus spends most of his time consulting with buyers and sellers, absent from me, and the household. He rarely sees Tydeus either. My merchant husband is making money from the war, which takes most of his time and attention. He usually eats elsewhere and comes home to sleep in the chamber he occupies as his own. His fleet of mercantile ships grows, but he is worried about their safety and so often keeps them moored in the port at Piraeus, surrounded by the high wall, except for short excursions to trustworthy areas.

Although he is rarely at home, Aegeus sporadically enjoys lavish symposiums in the larger first floor *andron* for his friends, their young *eromenos*, and *Hetaera*, well-educated, talented and beautiful high class prostitutes. Throughout the long nights I can hear the sounds of drunken laughter, a flute, and sometimes women singing.

After too many events like that, one night just after midnight I become angered. I creep down the stairs, listening at the *andron* entrance, at what is unmistakably the sound of lovemaking. I open the curtain, surprising all those in attendance. Aegeus is laying on a floor cushion, two Hetaeras tending to his erotic needs, while he lays in ecstasy. Several other men are likewise engaged, some with the other women, others with their adolescent lovers, the *eromenos*. A young *Hetaera* sits in the corner on a couch, singing a playful tune while accompanying herself on a lute. Wine bottles and half-empty wine glasses are abandoned everywhere, along with messy food platters.

"So, Husband!" I shout. "This is why you never come to my bed. You blame me, though you are impotent, and require the buying of whores. What a swine!"

Some men laugh uproariously at my melodramatic speech. Several of the *Hetaera* titter. There is no shame in the room. Only male sanction exists, to do as they wish.

"Wife, return to your room. We will not discuss this further. You are dismissed! Stay in your place, in your part of the house. This is mine and you are not welcome!" Aegeus returns to his pleasurable activity while the *Hetaera* women have scarcely moved, intent on their duties.

I exit, not knowing what to do or say. Laughter greets me again as I leave, burning with my own ignominy. I am his lawfully wedded wife, with no rights or privileges, except to observe such goings-on with abject powerlessness. I have married into male tyranny. Although Aegeus has massive wealth and power, I am but a slave to his whims and wishes.

After that night Aegeus seeks his own revenge, making sure that when I leave the villa to go to market, the Agora, I am accompanied by a caretaker *gynaikonomoi*, usually a male slave, during my childbearing years, as this is the custom for most young Greek wives. I am considered to be incapable of sexual continence and need to be strictly overseen by a *gynaikonomoi* during my childbearing years. I am insulted by the unreasonable Greek practice, yet I have no options.

Towards the end of summer, Aegeus invites me to the *oikos*, an unexpected occasion. "Selene," he says, referring to me by name. "My friends and I discuss you and your skills."

I shudder, remembering the appalling tableau I witnessed.

"Not those skills," he corrects me. "The ones having to do with Apollo. There is no reason to keep you locked up when you have abilities and can share them with others. We have need of you, especially now that we are unable to travel to Delphi to consult with your mother, Xanthippe, the Oracle."

I am gratified, yet wary.

"I therefore invite you to join us in the small *andron* once a week. If all goes well, I will increase the meetings to several times a week."

I stand quietly. I have been chastised and disciplined during my time at the villa and am loath to speak. Aegeus is worse than my mother could ever hope to be, while he holds the keys of my bondage.

"Well?" he queries. "Do you agree?"

"Do I have a choice to agree or not?"

"Of course, you do," he responds pleasantly.

"I would like to think about it first," I temporize.

"No! I want your answer this moment," he bullies me.

I wonder how I ever thought of him as a kind, generous man, but keep my mouth closed.

"The first meeting is scheduled in four days, when most of my friends can gather here."

"Will strong wine be served?" I inquire.

"No, only wine that is watered down." He turns abruptly and leaves me alone in the *oikos*. Our discussion is concluded.

The evening of the fourth day, as confirmed, I dress in my most beautiful *chiton* with geometric designs at the bottom and am escorted to his *andron*. The room is smaller than the other men's chamber, with fewer couches and tables, so men are jammed together. Nor is it as highly decorated as the larger *andron*, but rather is austere in comparison. Aegeus leads me to a chair. A scribe is seated on the floor to take notes, papyrus attached to a wooden board on his lap, reed pen in hand. Other men are already seated on couches or floor cushions. In all there are nine of us, including Aegeus. Everyone looks at me expectantly.

Aegeus introduces me. "Many of you know my wife, Lady Selene."

I nod politely and sit down on the empty chair.

"What you may not know is that she was in training to become the next Oracle at Delphi. Both her mother and grandmother were Oracles at that magnificent Temple. I offered her my hand in marriage. She accepted and I brought her here."

Several men grin in admiration for Aegeus.

"She has the ability to converse with Apollo. Not simply at the sacred spring in the *Adyton* of Delphi, but virtually any place and any time. She has been instrumental in war efforts, giving information in advance of the whereabouts of enemy troops and the outcome of land and sea battles."

A sprinkling of applause.

"My wife is here to answer your questions tonight. Cletus will take notes," indicating the scribe on the floor. "Who would like to be the first to begin?"

Timon stands. "I have won the toss of a coin," he states arrogantly. "I know the lady well. She sent many messages to help us in Athens." He nods then seats himself on his couch to begin. He is an influential Senator from Athens. Timon attended our wedding and was one of the men I saw in the large *andron*, engaged with a *Hetaera* that infamous night.

"Are you ready, Revered Seeress?"

"I am ready."

"Here is my question. My oldest son Aleksy is ill with palsy since birth. We have employed the most renowned physicians of Athens, but still he is sick. What can we do to cure him?"

I take a deep breath. "I am an honorable priestess of Apollo, and therefore must be candid at all times, even if it angers powerful men. Or my husband."

An audible gasp fills the small *andron.*

"Pray, Madame. Continue," rejoins Timon, gritting his teeth.

"Yes, Honored Sir. First, the son you speak of was birthed by a slave in your household. He is therefore the illegitimate son of you and the slave woman Gael. Aleksy is not the highborn son you claim. Indeed you have no living sons from your wife, Sabra."

Timon's mouth flies open in anger. "Stop this woman!"

Several men snigger.

One says, "Let her finish speaking the god's words, Timon. Now the truth is out at last, which has only been a rumor before tonight."

"She lies!"

"Noble Timon, please allow me to answer the question you pose to Apollo," I continue civilly.

"How dare you!" The Athenian nobleman abruptly leaves the *andron* in a rage, knocking over a small statue in offended retreat.

The men look at each other questioningly and then at Aegeus.

Aegeus comments wryly. "Would anyone else like to resume? Or are you all faint-hearted as women?"

"I'll go next," counters Erasmus, the man who had commented on Timon's reading. He squirms nervously in his chair, but proceeds. "I own much property in Plataea as well as in Athens. What does the god tell me about the future of my holdings?"

I didn't need to close my eyes as the answer leaps out at me. "Your property in Athens, Sir, is safe for the moment. But I encourage you to sell all the land in Plataea immediately before the Spartans take it over. Then buy it back after the war is over, at much lower prices. Thus increasing your wealth three-fold."

"Well done!" shouts another man, clapping Erasmus on the shoulder.

Erasmus grins at the information. "Apollo is a good businessman," he chuckles heartily.

The evening continues. Sometimes the information I give a man is unpleasant. Sometimes welcomed. While every man has a chance to question Apollo, questions and answers are written down by the scribe Cletus.

Aegeus says at closing. "If anyone wants a transcript of his questions and answers, Cletus will provide it."

The men leave, commenting to each other and joking, handing Aegeus jingling bags of coins as they depart.

Aegeus has hired me to channel Apollo, while intending to collect the proceeds himself!

"Aegeus," I speak softly, rising from my chair, hesitant to arouse his ire, yet determined in my goal. "I will take half of the proceeds from tonight. If you wish me to continue as your private Oracle, I will take fifty percent of every night henceforth as well."

He glares but doesn't speak. Perhaps he cannot believe I stand up to him in this matter.

"It is my right as a paid employee. You understand business. I do, too. I am not the slave of Apollo."

"We shall see."

"You do not want to be known as a trader who cannot be relied on, but defaults on his contracts." I hold out my hand for the pouches.

He reluctantly hands me three of the six pouches, as Timon did not pay for his consultation.

"Now we are truly partners," I say, weighing them in my hand. "In future, let us count out the coins first and divide those by half, rather than by pouch."

"Hmmmp," he comments, displeased but maintaining the agreement as an ethical dealer.

I return to my chamber and pour out the monies from the three pouches onto my mattress. One of them contains several Athenian owl coins, each worth four *drachmas*, plus other coins. A skilled craftsman would be paid one drachma per day so I received good wages for my evening's work. I return the coins to the pouches and hide them under some scrolls, saving them for an emergency. These coins are mine to keep as Aegeus buys all I personally require plus household goods.

* * *

As a final threat to an already unsettling year, plague returns that winter to Athens. We have begun to hear rumors before it spreads to the general population. Aegeus, as always organized and prepared, immediately packs all of us, himself, Melita, Tydeus and me, along with a few slaves, and hurries us aboard one of his ships moored at the harbor of Piraeus.

Twenty warships, *triremes*, are also anchored at Piraeus, each ship containing 170 rowers. "They are awaiting orders," Aegeus mentions to me as we pass.

His ship sails to the island of Naxos where he lived during the first plague. We are ushered by curtained litters to his superb seaside home. Although Naxos is more tropical than Athens, that day the weather is overcast and chilly when we arrive. We stay inside the gleaming white-washed house belonging to Aegeus until the weather grows warmer. Tydeus especially is bad-tempered at being walled in, while the turquoise Aegean Sea summons us to its gleaming shore.

Chapter 14

Naxos   Age 24   426 BC

In late summer of the 6th year of the war, both Peloponnesian *hoplites*, heavily armored, and the peltasts, light troops, totaling 3,000 men under the command of Eurylochus, march to Delphi. After a respite at Delphi, they continue on to Naupactus in northwest Greece. Fighting commences in areas surrounding Naupactus as well as at Olpae and Idomene. The Athenian fleet of 20 *triremes* led by Demosthenes blockade Olpae to prevent enemy troops from outnumbering Athenian forces.

* * *

When I acquire the latest news of Delphi, my first thought is of my mother, Xanthippe. What has become of her? Is she well? Does she continue to be the Oracle at Delphi? Did the Spartans confer with her as Oracle? Has my mother unwittingly become an enemy of Athens, including Tydeus and me? I must assume all is true. Apollo does not take sides in this war, but communes with all Oracles and Seers, delivering information to whatever questions are asked, only depending on the veracity of the Oracle or Seer.

I hear news that the citizens of Naupactus are endangered, which includes freed slaves and their children. Former Spartan slaves called *helots* could be recaptured and returned to servitude or even executed. Although I prefer to remain neutral, I am distressed at the fate of many innocent people and their children.

I do not like war. There is no honor in war. What honor can there be in killing harmless people? When Greeks soldiers, similar to athletes, compete using intellectual skill, initiative, even trickery, inoffensive men, women, and children are injured, enslaved, or killed on sophisticated playing fields that run with blood.

Those of us staying on Naxos had been anxious earlier in the year as Spartans were rumored to attack close at hand in the south, perhaps overrunning all of Attica. The only factor that would save Athens is the Great Wall. However, Athens and their allies were rescued by a series of earthquakes throughout Greece, which the Spartans interpreted as malevolent portents, and thus stopped their project to invade Attica. Meanwhile fighting continues elsewhere, sometimes between tribes, other times between traditional enemies and their allies.

* * *

News comes to us on Naxos, an island of the Cycladic chain, that Athens has purified Delos, a nearby sacred island, of all residents. Does purified mean murdered? Subjugated? Or simply exiled?

Next, Athens, the preeminent civilized city-state, attacks the blameless tiny isle of Melos, also close to Naxos. The Athenians ruthlessly raze Melos with massive troop deployment for no motive that I can discern. What has become of the civilizing effect of Athens? Is Athens becoming indistinguishable from war-like Sparta? Or was there never a distinction?

Residents of Naxos, who include wealthy Athenians and Thebans, as well as emissaries from countries outside Greece, wait, worry, and pray to their various gods.

* * *

We spend time outside his little villa, which faces west to the Aegean, relaxing on the open-air patio in the shade of the terrace roof held up by Doric marble columns. Stroll on the nearby beach. Observe the two young people at play. Look forward to savoring delicious meals in exquisitely decorated wooden bowls served on terracotta platters with geometric patterns burned into the pottery. After the excitement of living in our busy villa in Athens, we are bored, particularly Aegeus.

Near the shore the sea is a light blue/green like the foam Aphrodite appeared in at birth. Farther into the depths, the water appears dark blue. Placid waves move in and out rhythmically like the Earth goddess breathing. The air is cooler here than on the mainland because of the currents of sea air—Zephyrs—that blow past the island, although the sun is still blistering.

We especially take time out of every day to watch the sunset, as each evening the sky is radiant, glorious, and unique. The Muses, Goddesses of Art, decorate the broad sky with their own personal palette. According to Hesiod, Zeus and Mnemosyne are the legendary parents of the nine Muses. Further back in time, legend explains that the Muses originated from ancient Egypt, where Osiris recruited them, employing the nine sisters to teach the arts of civilization wherever he traveled.

Sunsets in this island paradise are spectacular and distinctive. Each evening has its own display, changing moment by moment. Some nights as the sun chariot of Apollo sets in the west, the sky appears to have caught on fire, while layers of oranges intertwine in the red firmament. Other nights the sky turns purple, while swirls of pinks and lavenders compete for beauty. On other evenings the sky becomes deep blue, while darkest blue hues mix with oranges and yellows. We immensely enjoy the Muses' shows of light and color until starry darkness intervenes, ruled by Urania, one of the nine sisters.

As we watch the ever-changing panorama of the darkening sky, I teach Melita and Tydeus the systematic set of functions assigned to the Muses: "Calliope (epic poetry); Clio (history); Euterpe (flutes and lyric poetry); Thalia (comedy and pastoral poetry); Melpomene (tragedy); Terpsichore (dance): Erato (love poetry); Polyhymnia (sacred poetry); and Urania (astronomy)."

"Tell us more," Melita implores me. She is budding into a young woman. Tydeus is young, immature, and quickly becomes disinterested in my teachings, more engrossed in the seashells he finds on the sand, than my words.

I continue. "The Muses are divine. Children, do you know that one can interpret information from Apollo, as does the Oracle at Delphi, by using poetry or verse?"

* * *

A donkey cart driven by a slave appears at our villa a few days after we arrive at Naxos. A close neighbor named Eudoxia, self-appointed social leader of Naxos, has come to introduce himself. Eudoxia is genial and ebullient, somewhat overweight, perhaps a devoted follower of Dionysus, and an impressive conversationalist.

Dinnertime approaches while Eudoxia hopes to wangle a dinner invitation. Aegeus invites the influential man to dine with him while the children and I eat in a separate area.

Eudoxia remains for a lavish meal, entertaining Aegeus about the sights to be found at Naxos. "There are Temples," he exclaims, "as exquisite as any in Attica. Temples to Hera and Demeter. There is an unfinished temple to Apollo on a hilltop, overlooking the Aegean, not far from here. A marble doorway called the Portara is at the top. Now that's a place to enjoy sunsets! Aegeus, you are staying at one of the most beautiful islands in Greece. Many things to see. The finest people, too."

I can hear his monologue from our small dining room. Eudoxia's eloquent voice carries clearly through the hallway.

"Then in the valley of Melanes is the Naxian marble quarry, famous throughout Greece, where exquisite marble is extracted for our temples and statues. A large carved marble statue of a young boy, a kouras, lies abandoned on the ground. Supposedly it was meant to be a statue of either Apollo or Dionysus. The statue cracked before it could be completed. You must come on a tour with me of the island. I will make sure to have my slaves prepare food for us on our short excursions."

"How long do you think it will take to do the tour?" Aegeus asks, ever practical.

"Oh. A day. Or a week. However much you want to take," he replies airily, waving a half-eaten drumstick in his hand. "Naxos is fairly small, so no more than two weeks. Unless you wish to lounge at every location. Visit every family. We have no lack of time here," he smiles. "Everyone is bored, like you. Looking for entertainment and diversion. One can sit on the sizzling beach for only so long, until one ends up looking like a steamed lobster from Xalkidiki."

I grin at the reference to food, obviously one of his favorite subjects. A noticeable epicurean. If only I could be allowed to sit at the dinner table with the two men. Eudoxia's conversation is spellbinding and entertaining. I am anxious for us to begin the tour he speaks of, to learn about this island. I may never be back here again. At heart I am an academic, hungry for learning, as well as a romantic.

"Young Tydeus may become restless and fidgety," Aegeus responds with concern.

"Then we will take the children only on short jaunts." Eudoxia neutralizes the problem. "No reason that everyone cannot enjoy himself while here, even the little ones."

"Possibly," Aegeus answers.

Then in a more serious tone, fortunately out of earshot of Melita and Tydeus, he asks Aegeus. "How long do you think the sickness will last in Athens, my dear friend? When might we return?"

"Previously the plague lasted more than a year, but less than two. How long have you been here at Naxos?"

"I came here in the course of the prior outbreak of the plague. My wife sickened and died in Athens during a short visit to our home before we could flee to Naxos. We had no children and she was my only family. Now I believe I am ready to go home soon. My funds are frightfully diminished, so I have no choice."

"You know about Pericles, of course?"

"Oh, yes. The illustrious man and his family. Perished."

"That was a tragedy," Aegeus nods solemnly.

"A pity. Such a pity. We need the likes of him now. A general, politician, and builder of great monuments. Tsk, tsk," he went on.

"Where do you live?" asks Aegeus, wanting to change the conversation.

"Outside Athens to the south. In Brauron. I also own a small villa in the city of Athens as well."

"Brauron near the Temple of Poseidon?"

"Yes, not far from that Temple overlooking the sea. Ah, what a splendid work of art it is. I was there during a festival for Poseidon." He gulps a mouthful of wine in remembrance. "Then I have my resort here on Naxos." Without pause, he continues. "I heard rumors that the Peloponnesians were planning to attack Attica this year, except that earthquakes stopped them."

"You have heard correctly, sir."

"What if they had despoiled Poseidon's temple and many others? Sparta and their allies are a worrisome throng, barbaric and uncivilized, fearful of omens and portents. Not at all like us rational Atticans," he brags. "Hahaha!"

"One can only hope that will not happen."

"We are orators and philosophers, an enlightened group, are we not? Not superstitious as they are, bred from infancy to become warriors." Without hesitation, he requests: "Could you pass the tzatziki and pita bread? And wine too of course."

"Please help yourself. It is my honor to celebrate you in my home."

"Thank you for your munificence, kind Aegeus of Athens." He tears off a small piece of chicken and stuffs it in his mouth. "We must bring your lovely wife on tour as well, dear sir," he mumbles, while attempting to swallow and talk at the same time.

"My wife would like that. She reads and studies constantly."

"Is she a scholar?"

"A self-taught student."

"Ah," he replies. "Unusual for a mere woman."

"Yes, very."

"How did that come about? If you don't mind my asking."

"She is the daughter and granddaughter of two Delphic Oracles. Her mother Xanthippe still lives in Delphi as the Pythia there. My wife, Selene, was in training to become the next Oracle and thus is well-educated."

"Ye, gods. What a story! An amazing heritage! I imagine you are honored."

Aegeus hesitates. "Yes, I am gratified. She will teach our children of course, so that I do not have to hire tutors."

"How many children do you have?"

"Only one son so far. I pray for more."

"Excellent. I hope the gods will be with you." He slaps Aegeus on the shoulder. "Well, my dear sir, I must be heading home. The light is fading fast, as it does here on the islands. My slave will need to see his way back. The moon is less than a quarter full tonight."

"Of course. Thank you for gracing our home."

"My pleasure. I look forward to more meetings. I will put together trips for us to take."

* * *

As promised, Eudoxia organizes lavish outings for us to tour around Naxos.

Against my wishes, Aegeus keeps Melita and Tydeus at home, while grudgingly allowing me to accompany them. "Be on your best behavior," he warns me.

On one of our tours, we stop for lunch at the home of Eudoxia. His home is lovely and refined.

"This villa is mostly the work of my wife, before she took sick and left me to live in the underworld. We often came here in the summer to avoid the heat of Brauron and Athens."

I murmur unobtrusively. "Some of your statues are unique, noble Eudoxia. I've never seen the like of them before."

"Ah, yes, dear lady." He turns to me in anticipation. "These figures and pottery are known as Cycladic art. Famous in these islands. Their culture is supposedly from the same or earlier time period as Krete and Mycenae." He picks up a triangular-shaped figurine carved out of marble. A woman from the minimal look of it, with bumps for breasts, and a v-shaped pubic area. "Would you care to examine it closer?"

"Please."

The figure is no bigger than my hand.

"Be cautious. This is rare and therefore priceless." He gingerly begins to hand it to me.

Aegeus is closely scrutinizing me and I hastily refuse. "Please hold it while I look at it. I do not want to damage so valuable an item."

Eudoxia smiles with the appreciation of an art collector then turns to Aegeus. "I would like to present you with this small statuette."

"I accept," Aegeus says without hesitation, "with humble thanks. I will display it with pleasure in Athens at my villa when I return." He continues. "Do you have others of its kind for sale?" Aegeus is eternally a merchant.

"Oh dear me, no, good sir. These pieces are extraordinary and I would never be able to name a price. My wife hand-picked every one you see here. Each was crafted by artisans that are long dead while honoring an impressive tradition in these islands. This one is my gift to you."

"Then I am greatly honored. The statue will be placed in prominence so that my friends can appreciate it."

"That will gratify me." Eudoxia glances at me, and winks. Greek propriety has been observed.

* * *

The year ends with overall success for Athenian forces.

The plague in Athens continues unrelentingly.

Chapter 15

APOLLO'S MESSAGE FOR AEGEUS   AGE 25   425 BC

As the sun rises at Naxos, Apollo communicates another war alert to me.

"Agis, King of Sparta, is readying his troops to invade Attica, while the plague still rages in Athens."

I make sure to give a written message to a slave boy, who traveled with us to Naxos. He delivers the missive immediately to Aegeus. As the god's communiques increase in number and intensity, I continue to send posts every day to my husband.

Studying scrolls while lounging in the *gyneceum* is my daily custom. No new ones are able to penetrate through enemy lines, so I review those I have already studied since our stay in Naxos, trying not to crumple the precious edges or tear the papyrus.

Tydeus is playing on the floor with Melita, rolling and tumbling over her in delight. She tickles him just to hear him giggle. I smile with enjoyment at the happy sounds of the children.

"Wife," Aegeus seeks me out in the *gyneceum* in the afternoon. "Anything interesting?" he casually asks about the scroll without really wanting an answer. He obviously wants to talk to me.

"What are you doing in here?" I reproach him. "As you know, the *gyneceum* is only for women and children."

"I want to discuss something of importance with you."

"This is not a good time or place, Aegeus. Perhaps we can make an appointment for later in the evening."

"After dinner? In the *oikos*? Without the children?"

"Yes, all right," I reply and return to my scroll. I peek at him over the papyrus. He looks displeased as he departs the woman's space. Being resolute is the only way I can gain self-respect.

The slave cook prepares freshly-caught *lavraki*, sea bass, for dinner along with a stew of dried fava beans, garlic, and greens. I remember the delicious octapodi and barbouni Aegeus had kindly brought to my family at Delphi from Athens. What happened to that man?

After our mouthwatering dinner, I stroll leisurely into the *oikos*. Aegeus is waiting for me, tapping his foot impatiently.

"I am here, husband," I announce and sit on a foldable stool. Not comfortable, but I don't plan to stay long.

"I would like to set up meetings with you and Apollo again, as we did in Athens."

"I am willing to do so, if that is your pleasure."

"Splendid," he beams.

"However, I would like to make a new arrangement in regard to meetings."

"What is that?" He leans towards me, startled at my umbrage. "What new arrangement?"

"From this day forward I ask for 75 percent of the proceeds. This new agreement is appropriate as I do all the work while you and the other men lounge around, listening, drinking watered wine, and making jokes, sometimes at my expense."

"Without me there would be no gatherings," he argues.

"Without me there would be no messages. Therefore, no point in gathering," I counter without raising my voice.

I have struck a vital chord in him as he snorts and snuffles with ill-temper. He is incensed at my bargaining with him, a trade he is sure to lose if he persists on having his way.

I gracefully tease at the fabric of my stylish pink silk *chiton*, paying him no attention.

"What game are you playing, Selene?" he probes, obviously infuriated.

"No game, husband. Only seeking fairness in business, as you do yourself."

"Very well, then," he answers with ire. "You have me at a disadvantage."

"Do I?" I respond smoothly. "Do we have a contract then?"

"Yes, yes, a contract."

"When is this first meeting to take place?"

"Tomorrow night," then Aegeus leaves, annoyed, but with our agreement firmly in place.

Evening arrives and so do many young and old men. They are shown into the *oikos*, the only chamber with enough room for all of them. The ones who arrive early sit on chairs or stools, among them my husband's new friend Eudoxia. The rest are forced to take seats on the hard floor. Aegeus orders a slave to bring cushions from other rooms for comfort. The *oikos* is crowded with warm bodies, some smelling of garlic, all of them talking and wound up. Slaves light oil lamps as darkness falls.

I take a seat at the far end of the rectangular room, away from the main door, dressed demurely in an unembellished yellow *chiton* with a yellow veil covering my hair and shoulders. A female slave has worked for hours dressing my hair in the latest fashion. I wear the necklace with the sacred honeybee pendant that Aegeus gave me at our wedding celebration. Wordlessly I wait for the bantering to end, so I may begin.

Aegeus motions with his hand, and the room is suddenly silent. He briefly introduces me as he did in Athens. The men seated in this room are fabulously wealthy, powerful, and hail from all over Greece, several from Ionia, and other distant places as well. They are used to being attended upon their inclination and are impatient.

"Gentlemen," I begin. "Lords of the Universe. Purveyors of the goods of the world. I beg your kind indulgence."

The men glance at each other proudly, not realizing I am mocking them.

I move the filmy yellow veil further over my face. I feel naked in this propitious gathering and have a sudden urge to leave. But I stay. "Except for Eudoxia, I do not recognize any of your faces," I begin. "Have any of you been to see the Pythia at Delphi?"

Several raise their hands.

"You then understand what an Oracle may do?"

They nod their heads.

"Give information," one shouts so that others can hear.

"That is correct. Then a Priest of Apollo digests the information the Pythia gives, translates it into verse, and offers it to the seeker."

"Is that what you do?" a younger man inquires.

"No. Both my mother and grandmother were Delphic Oracles, and I trained for most of my life to do the same." Now it is my turn to feel pride. "My grandmother died a few years ago, but my mother is still the Pythia in attendance, seated in the *Adyton* breathing the vapors of the sacred space and passing on Apollo's messages. I have never been on Apollo's throne in a hallucinatory state. Rather I remain wide awake, seated before you. With ease I hear and feel the god's words, sometimes get visions, and have done so since I was a girl. I then speak honestly and plainly, whatever comes to me from the god. No translation is needed."

"A woman's place is in the *gyneceum*, not in the *oikos* of Aegeus, acting as an equal to men, saying whatever gibberish may come into her deceitful head," a dissenting voice is heard.

"Who speaks?" I ask. No one volunteers.

Eudoxia pipes up on my behalf. "Let the Seer speak without further insult. Those who are not at ease may leave."

All the men remain unmoving.

"Thank you," I murmur to Eudoxia then continue. "Apollo honors me like no other man or woman. The god gives me numerous messages during this terrible war, which others—those with more civility than the person who commented—are able to use. The messages are intended to prevent bloodshed, skirmishes, and battles, along with revealing troops and cavalry ready to pounce upon innocent citizens and murder courageous *hoplites*, as well as to win battles. Does that sound like gibberish to you? The formidable men who receive these many messages from me take them to heart and prevent carnage to Athens, Thebes, throughout Attica and Greece, and upon the sea."

Eudoxia nods at me.

The chamber is silenced. Where do my words come from? I have never spoke in such a compelling, resolute, and effectual way as tonight. The feeling of power emanates from within me. Pericles, once a famous orator in the Forum, comes to mind.

"Sirs. What is wisdom and from whose lips do we trust wise words? We are in a war celebrating Ambition which often leads to Injustice, while I think it is best to honor Equality in all human affairs, both in war and peace. I have studied scrolls of many articulate and wise men," I inform them.

"Here is a quote from the great Euripides:
My son Eteocles, old age is not
a total misery. Experience helps.
Sometimes we can speak wiser than the young.
Why do you seek after the goddess Ambition?
The worst of all; this goddess is Injustice.
Often she comes to happy homes and cities,

and when she leaves, she has destroyed their owners,
she after whom you rave. It's better, child,
to honor Equality who ties friends to friends…"

My face warms with self-consciousness. Several in the audience applaud my words or those of Euripides.

I continue. "I tell you friends from Naxos, Athens, Thebes, Sparta, or from wherever you hail. Apollo's words fall on equal ears, in absolute truth, from these humble lips, to answer your questions and your prayers. I do not sit on a three-legged throne. I do not breathe in hallucinatory emissions meant to stimulate Apollo's messages. The god's words come unmistakably through me. All the while I am lucid and wide-awake. I offer you the opportunity tonight to ask your own significant questions. Apollo will reply clearly and concisely. Be sure to word your questions carefully."

They are all staring at me. In anger? Respect?

"Who would like to begin?"

"I would," speaks Aegeus, surprising everyone in the gathering, including me. He has drunk much wine and rises unsteadily to his feet. "Lady Selene. I have a painful question that has distressed me for some time. I have longed for a message from Apollo and hope that the god hears me tonight and grants me knowledge."

"Honorable Aegeus. What is your question?" I inquire courteously. My husband has never been as vulnerable as he is in this moment.

"Reverend Selene, Seer of Great Farsightedness. Tell me. Where is Heraclius? What has become of him? Is he dead or alive? I miss him dreadfully."

Gasps of confusion fill the *oikos*. Men turn to one another and mutter.

Stunned, I struggle to continue. "Dearest Sir. Your questions are honorable and heart-felt," I begin. "You were an *erastes* to Heraclius, your *eromenos*. This was no light relationship but one in which the two of you were deeply bonded. In Thebes these men go into battle with their lovers at their sides. Why can they not be united as a man and a woman are joined in matrimony? In a better world, you and Heraclius could have married and lived together until old age. A family created by love and friendship, where Heraclius would have inherited your wealth. This we do not yet have in Greece. This kind of relationship is whispered of in dark corners. Some may snigger at a lifelong passion between two men. I do not. I saw your devotion and friendship with each other at close hand. More than a father and son, but deep as a marriage similar to that of a man and woman, yet without being able to tie those bonds because of our society's restraints. Aegeus, I can only imagine your turmoil, loss, and grief."

Aegeus leans forward, listening intently, obviously transported by my heartfelt words, which deeply affect him. Although he and I have problems, I do not hate him. He is the adopted father of Tydeus, my son with Heraclius. Compassion runs through me tonight, for which I'm grateful. Can we reside together in his house without malice? I close my eyes for a few moments. Surprising words come from Apollo as low-pitched, rather than my own feminine voice.

"Heraclius lives," Apollo announces through me. "He is not dead, though profoundly wounded. He lives in darkness. Sometime soon he will emerge from obscurity to head a family. Selene will find him, when it is time for him to be found."

Aegeus shouts. "Heraclius! He lives! He will return!"

I stand up and walk over to my husband. "I'm sorry Aegeus. I didn't understand your true feelings before tonight."

"Thank you." His eyes glow with feeling.

"I hope your questions were answered with the kindness and clarity as you hoped."

"Yes," he gulps.

As a man he is uncomfortable with open displays of emotion, preferring rational, practical concerns. His is a shocking display, which the other men try to sort out for themselves.

An intermission takes place. A round of watered wine is served, along with fruit, dates, and nuts. His friends step outside to the courtyard, sipping and murmuring with embarrassment. The others aren't ready to experience their own depths of honesty and emotion. Shortly after intermission, all the guests including Eudoxia depart, nodding at Aegeus as they do so.

After the men have left, he looks sadly at me. "I thought I could keep my promise to marry you. I tried for his sake and his child. I wanted to have a family and be a respected member of society. But now I have become an aberration. Please forgive me, Selene."

"I love him, too," I murmur.

He is quite drunk with wine and emotion. "Selene, you are more magnificent every time I see you conducting one of these meetings with Apollo. Tonight it was as if the god himself was speaking through your lips. Touching all of us. This is your great gift. I'm sorry I have been an unkind husband, keeping you away from yourself and your work, locking you away. Punishing you because you are not Heraclius. That you are not a man, but an insignificant woman. I promise to try better in the future."

I place my hand kindly on his. "We can transform, husband. Do you see that? It is possible we can begin again, to attempt to be better partners than before."

"I'm willing."

"From what Apollo said tonight, I am supposed to go search for Heraclius at some point in the future."

"By yourself?"

"Perhaps I could travel with a group of *hoplites* on horseback to cover the most ground in the shortest time, while you care for Tydeus."

"You would bring Heraclius home to me?"

"Yes, husband, if that is the command from Apollo."

"Thank you, Selene." He kisses me tenderly on the cheek. Not a kiss of passion but of gratitude. "Sleep with me tonight. I am utterly lonely."

"I will. I am, too."

I check on Tydeus who is sleeping soundly before I meet Aegeus in my bedchamber. Melita sits on the floor near the child's bed, holding his hand while he sleeps, her head on the mattress, breathing softly. She is no longer his nurse but elder sister. The two youngsters have become family.

The slaves are already at work cleaning the house. I leave them to their duties and join Aegeus in my large bedchamber. He lays in bed naked, awake, waiting for me. Shyly I undress with my back to him and then swiftly get under the silken coverlet. He takes me into his arms. I sigh with relief and appreciation. Touch is essential to life while I have been slowly dying from its lack.

"My dear Selene. Love is complicated. Heraclius should never have asked me to marry you. I aspired to do as he asked. I wanted to make him happy. I married you on his behalf. I've tried to be a good husband."

"I understand. We both love him and want his love." I sigh and snuggle up to Aegeus. Our bodies are close but our hearts soar infinities away from each other, beating contrarily.

As the wine's effects diminish he whispers. "It is just a rumor, Selene."

"What is a rumor?"

"Heraclius cannot be alive. People at Naxos and Athens have heard reports of his death. Apollo lies to you."

"Apollo never lies."

"Then you are lying to me. You plan to run away, leave me, at the first opportunity." He is unexpectedly distraught.

Startled, I sit up next to him, my hand on his arm. "Oh, Aegeus. I would never do that. Please believe me."

"You are unhappy with me. With our life together." Angry now, he turns away from me, his arm cradling his head, a radical alteration from his earlier emotions.

Somehow I dare to speak to his questioning. "I cannot lie. Nothing can be hidden in a family or between two people in a marriage. You are correct. I am unhappy."

"My marriage with you is a sham. How can I undo this damage?" he slurs, again facing me, his eyes unfriendly and distant.

"I don't know, Aegeus. What do you want from me? What can I give you?"

"Every time I look at you, I wish to gaze upon Heraclius instead. I cannot pretend love with you. My body does not lie."

"Is that why…"

"Yes. Although oddly enough I can perform with a *Hetaera*. When I am with my friends. Having drunk too much wine. Then I can forget and fantasize."

"Oh," I answer forlornly. "Is there nothing left for me?"

"I will care for you and Tydeus, as I have promised. Ours is empty like many of the marriages in Athens." He falls asleep next to me, avoiding touching me.

I awake when the rays of the sun peek through the curtains of the window. Outside I can hear the surf break against the sand in its ceaseless rhythm. Aegeus has already left the bed.

"Heraclius," I whisper softly, as if he can hear me. "I have one purpose left. I must locate you if you are indeed among the living."

Apollo sends me a reassuring message. "I tell you truth, Selene. Heraclius lives. You will find him."

* * *

Aegeus invites guests to the beach house many times, to ask their own questions and listen to messages from Apollo. Never again does he bring up the issue of Heraclius. Meanwhile, I hoard my wages in anticipation of a journey that Apollo revealed—to find Heraclius.

Chapter 16

IANTHE AND KRITON   AGE 26   424 BC

War rages on for the 8th exhausting year.

* * *

We receive word that no one has died from the plague in over two months. Therefore, physicians announce that Athens is safe for residents to return home. However, a drought has been fulminating in place of the disease. The snow failed to fall adequately in winter, while spring rains have been light and generally ineffectual. Everywhere trees are beginning to perish of thirst.

Are the gods angry with us for fighting each other instead of living peacefully?

Towards the end of summer, going into the period of *pyanepsion*, September and October, we— Aegeus, myself, Tydeus, Melita and the slaves—return to the villa in Athens via his ship. When we are conveyed by slave carts from Piraeus, everywhere the buildings of Athens are covered with dust and grime, the walls grey instead of gleaming white.

His elegant, beautiful house is in chaos. Starving, homeless people had taken residence in the villa but were removed by authorities before we returned. His house slaves have all vanished, more afraid of the plague than of being caught and punished. Otherwise they would have protected the house from interlopers.

Clothing, statues, cooking implements and most items of value are gone. Beautiful chitons I left behind have been stolen. No one can read, so the scrolls are left untouched, but I took my pouches stuffed with coins and my precious necklace to Naxos. Cooking fires burned in the smaller *andron*, which needs to be scoured clean. Strangers slept in our beds. Furniture has been carelessly damaged or else hauled away.

The garden has not been tended to since the slaves' disappearance, while many trees and plants have withered without extra water. Weeds thickly grow everywhere. Aegeus is dismayed at the destruction.

I know his penchant for organization and I fear not. "You will repair and decorate the house and garden better than before," I tell him. "They are simply possessions and can be replaced."

"But they were my possessions," he corrects me, angry and hurt. "My home was vandalized by thugs and many items cannot be replaced. Even my statue of Heraclius is cracked."

"Husband, those people had nowhere to go during the plague. Your villa was a refuge, a safe haven."

"Hmmmp," is his only answer.

"What would we have done without you, your money, and your small villa on Naxos? Think, Aegeus. And Tydeus? What would a small poor child have done who was caught between war and plague?"

"You are right, Selene," he agrees reluctantly. "I will buy more slaves at the market in order to rebuild."

"Those men, women, and children at the market are enemies of Attica, sometimes soldiers, but mostly innocent civilians, who have been captured and enslaved by Athens. Families can be split apart and sold separately!" I exclaim.

"I will endeavor to keep entire families together. They will work better that way," he advises me.

"I do not like slavery at all," I rejoin. "Could you hire free men instead?"

"They cost a lot of money."

"Yes, but you do not have entitlement to possess people. They have the right to live their lives as they wish. I have been a slave and I know what it is like."

"You were never a slave," he reprimands me.

"Yes, I was and am. Just slavery of a different sort," I dispute. "Why don't you free your other slaves as well, Aegeus. They will be happy to stay here as it has been their home for years."

"The cost of replacing furniture, household items, statues, and art will be enormous," he complains. "I need slaves."

"You have made a fortune already from the war. So it will balance out in your ledger."

In the end, Aegeus acquiesces to my logic and hires servants instead of buying slaves, freeing those who are already slaves. He engages workers to remodel the slave quarters into apartments for servants.

He grumbles. "It will take me a long time to acquire my things again."

"Hire a worker to be your assistant." An idea occurs to me. "Tydeus would love to go auctions and markets with you. He is six now, old enough now to appreciate being of help while spending time with you. You will be teaching him a valuable trade as well."

"That is a good idea," he agrees. "The only item I can never replace is the statue of Heraclius. He modeled for it himself."

"It is unfortunate, but at least the statue is mostly in one piece, just chipped here and there."

I barely see my husband throughout the fall and winter. He travels, locates, bargains, and buys lovely and functional pieces of furniture, much needed household items, and art. He brings his son Tydeus with him, while Melita stays home with me. I've never seen Tydeus happier than when spending time with his adopted father.

"The boy has a good eye for beauty as well as value," Aegeus comments to me. "I will teach him to negotiate when he is a little older."

I'm delighted for my son but sad for myself. I have a husband in name only. We spend virtually no time together and are distant emotionally as well. I continue to study and learn, now writing my own thoughts and creating poetry on scrolls. But scrolls are not people. I crave intimacy while mostly confined in my own home. At least in Delphi I lived in a cave of my own choosing without being guarded like a prisoner.

Just before spring Aegeus makes contact with me after months of ignoring me. "How do you judge the improvements and purchases Tydeus and I have made? Did you notice statues carved from Naxian marble?"

"They are exquisite, husband. Greek art is the finest in the world. You must have a banquet, to show off the villa in its splendor once again."

"That is a wonderful idea," he exclaims.

The banquet is attended by many prominent citizens and their wives. Aegeus proudly shows off the villa, introducing Tydeus as his assistant. The boy swells with pride.

Afterwards Aegeus decides he will again commence the readings with Apollo. He crowds people into the large *oikos*, while even more individuals clamor to attend. Athens knows me as Selene. When I go to the Agora, people recognize me and call my name, or jostle to get close enough to touch my veil. Yet I am a captive of this society and for being female.

Just before the weather turns hot, when people leave Athens for a cooler locale, Aegeus determines he will arrange a symposium as he used to do. Invitations go out. His friends, their young lovers, *eromenos*, as well as *Hetaera* will attend. In his excitement Aegeus appears younger and more vibrant than I have seen him in seasons.

Unlike the banquet and the readings, I dread the symposium and remember the shocking night of another symposium with great clarity. I plan to confine myself to my room with my scrolls and try to sleep. Perhaps drink some strong wine to disengage my mind. Put wool plugs in my ears to drown out unwelcome sounds.

Food and wine is ordered and delivered. Servants have been cooking for days. Guests will be served delectable items. The villa is cleaned and swept. The gardens are growing again, being irrigated and tended by our faithful servants. Trees and bushes have been replaced and some are fruiting. All is in readiness.

The symposium is scheduled during the evening of a full moon, which lights up the garden with its eerie luminescence. Full moon is a fantastical time of the month. Lunacy is thought to be caused by the moon. Will there be madness this night?

Preparations have been finalized and guests will soon arrive. I stand in the *oikos* near the front entrance, dressed in a white *chiton*, light *chlamys* and veil, bathed in moonlight. "You are Selene, the moon goddess," my husband jokes as he walks by.

"That is what Heraclius called me," I murmur. Aegeus doesn't hear me but moves quickly past on his way to the large *andron*. Suddenly I experience horrifying sensations. Fear. Disgust. Foreboding. My feelings are your messages, Apollo.

Stunned by Apollo's unwelcome communication I cannot move from the front door and stand frozen like one of his statues. What is going to happen? Something dreadful.

Visitors arrive. I recognize Timon, who arrogantly walks by, shunning me. Others enter who have attended my readings. Several adolescent boys with smooth cheeks, hardly old enough to grow whiskers, accompany them. None of them acknowledge my presence. They are in their own separate world from which I am excluded and non-existent. I am a woman.

Then a tall *Hetaera* arrives. She appears to be from the East, with black hair, high cheekbones, and a slender body, with eyes shrouded by luxurious, dark lashes made thicker with soot. The woman is exotically dressed in multiple lavender veils with a matching *chiton* and *chlamys*. Her face is painted with white lead and her cheeks are rouged. Breasts beneath her nearly transparent clothing are small but firm, nipples prominent and inviting.

As she passes me, I observe that she has a physique like an athlete. Her long legs and arms bulge with muscles while her belly is flat and taut. What is most striking are her eyes. They are violet, the color of hyacinths in the spring, a color I have never seen before in a person. She is beyond stunning. The *Hetaera* is a vision of exquisite but cold, unapproachable loveliness.

She glances critically, looking at me as if I am a reviled piece of furniture. She reminds me of a cobra, upright, hood poised, ready to strike.

At that moment Aegeus appears from the *andron*. "Ianthe," he croons her name. They have obviously met before. He takes her muscular arm and guides her into the *andron*.

I am sickened. I run from the *oikos*, through the small *andron*, up the stairs, through the hall, to my room, for protection. Ianthe of the violet eyes. Who or what is she?

* * *

My feelings are indeed Apollo's message.

Ianthe spends the night of the symposium in his house, but does not leave in the morning with the others. Aegeus installs her in the extra bedroom next to my own. Slaves transport her possessions and clothing to her. Since all the rooms adjoin in the villa, she and her possessions must pass through my bedroom and closet in order to get to hers. Furthermore, she must walk through my room to go anywhere else in the house, including outside to the garden and lavatory. Aegeus must walk through my and adjoining bedrooms to arrive in Ianthe's room as well. All sounds carry from her room to mine, including those of an intimate nature.

I shudder with repugnance. Repulsed I hide in the *gyneceum* on the second floor, with its own separate door, thus avoiding my chamber, my husband, and his strange lover.

"Aegeus," I attempt to corner my husband in the courtyard several days later. "I have been looking for you."

He seems cheerful and happy. "Wife." He smiles broadly.

"Do not call me that!" I blurt.

"Is that not your title?"

"I am no longer your wife. I cannot tolerate this situation one more moment longer. What are you thinking?"

"Oh. You mean Ianthe?" he responds casually.

"Do not sport with me. I am offended beyond redemption. I thought we, you and I, were going to try harder as husband and wife."

"We have nothing. Our marriage is fruitless. Therefore, I have taken Ianthe as my concubine," he continues.

"What? This is intolerable, Aegeus. I have put up with a lot from you but you have gone too far this time."

"It is perfectly acceptable," he persists.

"Not with me!"

"All my friends in Athens have a concubine. Do you lack for anything as my wife?"

"Yes. I lack peace and love."

"How dare you speak thus!" his voice raises.

"This is my final word, Aegeus. Either she goes. Or I go!"

"Then leave!" he shouts. "I love her. As I've never loved anyone since Heraclius! You are nothing to me, Selene." He marches through the garden, back to the inner house, and thus to Ianthe's chamber.

Shaking with anger and grief, I return to the gyneceum. At least he cannot follow me to the women's chamber. I must think. Plan. What shall I do? My mind whirls.

What have I been studying all these years? Scrolls primarily written by men. For men. How to treat women. How to regard women. Women are nonentities. Meaningless as a spider on the wall, to be squashed if necessary.

I change into a linen *peplos*, veil myself, and throw an opaque *chlamys* over me, to disguise myself. The only place I can think of is the market, the Agora. What do I hope to discover there? My salvation.

I walk the dusty streets without a *gynaikonomoi* guarding me, hugging the *chlamys* close to me, hiding my face with the veil. No one yet recognizes me, for which I am grateful.

When I arrive at the Agora I see some women I met at the banquet. They are accompanied by their own slave *gynaikonomoi*, guarding them from sexual incontinence, to prevent them from impropriety.

Men are the ones who are sexually incontinent. Morally as well. Women are merely property to be watched over, lest someone steal them. Like the vagrants who lived at the villa during the plague, who stole urns and baskets, infuriating Aegeus.

I spot a man I know from the readings at the villa, although I have never spoken to him. It is Cletus, the scribe. "Cletus!' I cry out in desperation.

He looks up and sees me. "Lady Selene?" He walks over to me, glancing furtively over his shoulder.

I hardly recognize him without his scrolls and pen. "Yes, Cletus, it is me."

"Why are you here? Disguised like that?"

"I am in trouble, Cletus."

He frowns. "I cannot help you, Lady. You know that. You must ask your husband."

"My husband is the problem," I continue. I describe my quarrels with Aegeus. The symposium. The strange woman Ianthe and her being established as Aegeus' concubine. My craving to run away from home, ending up at the Agora with no means of escape.

"Do you not know?" he asks sympathetically.

"Know what?"

"Ianthe is a hermaphrodite. With both a man's and a woman's physical characteristics."

"Breasts, vulva, and a penis? With an athlete's body!"

"Yes," he admits. "Although being a hermaphrodite is sacred to the gods. They are considered sons and daughters of Hermes and Aphrodite."

"No wonder," I breathe, lowering my voice to avoid being overheard. "Aegeus seems happier than ever with that creature as a lover." I pull my veil closer. "Cletus," I continue. "Is there someone who can get me away from Athens? I must find Heraclius. Apollo has told me that I would find Heraclius when it was time. It is time, Cletus."

The scribe looks around to make sure no one can eavesdrop. "Perhaps. There is a man named Kriton, a soldier. He is part of a small group of *hoplites* who serve as mercenaries, going where they are paid. Kriton is a blameless man, honest, and serves a useful function."

"He sounds perfect. Do you know where he stays? Is he in Athens?"

"I will have to ask around. I do not know any other details."

"Could you come see me at the villa when you get the information? Possibly talk to Kriton first?"

"It is dangerous for me, Lady Selene. My livelihood as a scribe would be at stake. Perhaps worse."

"That is true." I bite my lip pensively.

"My brother could see you in my place. He is not well known in Athens."

"Would you do that, Cletus?" I exclaim with relief.

"Yes, I will do that," he agrees. "Come to the Agora tomorrow at this time. My brother will be here. His name is Bion. Bring money." With that Cletus hurries away.

I only have to wait one more day with the violet-eyed reptile in my house. I walk slowly home, not wanting to be there any longer than is required.

Then I remember Tydeus. What about Tydeus? I will have to leave him. I have no choice. Aegeus loves him and Melita will care for him, so he will be safe.

I hide in the gyneceum, hoping that the man/woman snake does not slither into my sanctuary. I tell Melita nothing, protecting her and Tydeus from the wrath of Aegeus. With luck Aegeus will not even miss me.

I do not change my clothes, but sleep fitfully, still dressed, on a cushion in the gyneceum.

I wake to one word. Money! I sneak noiselessly into my bedroom from the hallway and locate pouches I have hidden under a stack of scrolls. Coins I earned from readings. I get out my reed shopping basket, stuff the pouches in it, covering them over with several of my favorite scrolls. Then I procure the sacred bee necklace Aegeus gave me at our wedding, packaging it carefully and hiding it too in the basket. From the *oikos*, I obtain the Cycladic marble figurine that Eudoxia gifted us, wrap it tightly in a sturdy cloth, and place it at the bottom of the bag. Then wait.

Finally it is time to go the Agora. To obtain deliverance. I am exultant. My feelings are Apollo's messages.

The sun is hot. I sweat profusely. A column from the nearby Temple of Hephaestus provides some shade.

After some time elapses, a man walks over to me. "I am Bion," he says simply. "Are you Selene?"

"Yes."

He hands me a note on a bit of papyrus then departs.

The note says, "Kriton can meet you now. He is in the crowd. Look for a *hoplite* in light armor."

I spot him. A soldier wearing a red *chlamys*.

The *hoplite* nods at me briefly and approaches, speaking quietly. "You are Lady Selene?"

"Yes."

"I am Kriton. Come with me."

"Now?"

"It is your only hope. Follow well behind me, but keep me in your sight." He turns and walks away from the dusty crowd through narrow, curving streets.

"What choice do I have, Apollo?" I follow Kriton as instructed. My heart is pounding. Not far from the Agora I find the *hoplite* waiting with men and horses.

"We leave Athens at once. My men and I have horses. One is for you. We have food as well. Put this *chlamys* and helmet on. Tuck your hair underneath. Do not look up nor speak to anyone. Hold on tight."

After I don the two items, he helps me onto the horse, securely fastens my reed basket to my waist, then our group canters nonchalantly to the city limits of Athens. The Great Wall looms ahead. After passing through the western gate of Dipytos, we gallop away, riding fast, north towards Thebes, the largest city in Boeotia, ally of Sparta.

"How do we avoid Peloponnesians?" I shout, my legs tightly wrapped around my horse, holding the reins and mane tightly.

"We are mercenaries," Kriton yells back. "We work for everyone. We are beholden to no one."

I am relieved that I have coins and my necklace.

* * *

Aegeus has an official family and is therefore acceptable in Athenian society. His culture believes having a concubine is normal and even praiseworthy for a wealthy man, but I cannot remain in bondage any longer. Besides, I need to find Heraclius.

Aegeus will mostly likely complain to his friends in the *andron*, sentiments similar to what Homer penned about Helen in The Odyssey:

"That callous woman,
too faithless to keep her lord and master's house…"

Chapter 17

THEBES   AGE 27   423 BC

9th year of war. Athens and Sparta agree upon a one year truce between them. Yet military campaigns continue without ceasefire throughout Greece between their respective allies, both on sea and land.

* * *

That night Kriton, the *hoplites* and I camp in their ramshackle tents on the plain of Boeotia. There may be troops nearby. We have no way of knowing, because I have not received warnings from Apollo. Athens is far to the southeast. The men light campfires and we cook old meat, tough as the leather of our sandals.

"Is there nothing else to eat?" I ask plaintively.

"Not presently," replies Kriton. "We will get to Thebes tomorrow."

"I thought you said we have food."

"This is food," he says with a wry grin.

I chew ineffectively for a while then spit out the mouthful. My stomach growls with hunger. I ignore it. "I wish I was like the horses, able to eat grass."

Kriton laughs, amused at my comment. "I often wish I was a horse, for many reasons."

"Why is that?" I ask then add, "I had no idea you enjoy humor. You seem like a most serious man to me."

"The situation may be serious yet absurd contradictions whirl within my mind." He grins.

"You speak like a philosopher."

"I am, in my own humble way."

I warm to the subject. "Have you read Socrates or Acrion?"

"I am sorry, my Lady, I have not. I have no scrolls nor time either. Perhaps you can tell me about their writings when we get to Thebes."

A philosophical soldier? "I would like that. I have a few scrolls with me, which I can read to you."

"That would be enjoyable. May I ask you something?"

"Yes, please go ahead."

"Cletus tells me that you are a famous Seer. Also that you are related to the Oracles of Delphi. Furthermore, that in Athens you were paid handsomely to provide messages from the god. Are those things true?"

"I was born in Delphi. My mother is an Oracle. My grandmother died not long ago and was also an Oracle most of her life. I was trained to be an Oracle but life intervened."

"As life often does," he comments wisely.

"I have been able to hear, feel, and see Apollo since I was a child."

"You have a wonderful, although terrible, gift."

I am fascinated at how Kriton swiftly contemplates what I say then comes up with either a witty or provocative rejoinder.

"So your family is venerated and distinguished. Therefore, I must call you Madame Selene of Delphi or Reverend Seeress. I beg your pardon if I have been crude in my manners."

"Are you teasing me?" I giggle unpredictably. "Please simply call me Selene. Perhaps I should call you by a title like Commander? After all, you rescued me and are in charge of these *hoplites*. As such you are in command."

"Would you relate to me the events that led me to rescue you?"

"I think you would find them of little consequence."

"Let me be the judge of that."

The rest of the *hoplites* have gone to their tents to sleep, while Kriton and I sit by the dying fire, enjoying our curious conversation. Thunder periodically booms in a distance then jagged lightning illuminates the night sky.

Surreptitiously I examine Kriton. His brown hair is quite long, gathered in back with a cord to keep it manageable. He has friendly brown eyes, with creases around them from years of squinting, being outside in the elements. He smiles easily and often, showing strong white teeth, the lines around his mouth deeply etched. His trustworthy face is set off by a brown beard and mustache, portions interspersed with grey. The soldier is brawny, not necessarily an attractive man, but easy to look at. I smile to myself.

"Now it is your turn for humor, Lady. What thought prompted your smile just now?"

"I did not know I would be rescued by a soldier, then have a philosophical discussion with him in the dead of night, in the middle of nowhere."

"You have a point," he hoots. His laughter is spontaneous and pleasing. "So tell me your story, Lady Selene. Madame Seer."

I sigh. "The story is commonplace. It is about a man."

"Of course. Your husband?"

"Yes, and another man too."

"Ah, I begin to apprehend complications. We will talk again on this subject at a later time. It is late."

"I have a question for you, Kriton."

"What is that?"

"Why aren't you and your men wearing greaves?"

"I thought your question would be philosophical!" He chortles.

"Leg armor has been deemed obsolete since the war began." He stands up and helps me to my feet, then walks me to my tent. "Lady Selene. August Seeress. I wish you a pleasant sleep and peaceful dreams."

"Thank you." I push open the flap and enter. I don't remove my clothing but lay down on a blanket, pulling another one over me, both provided by the *hoplites*. Exhaustion helps me sleep.

I am disturbed before dawn at a scratching at my tent. It is Kriton.

"We must leave at daybreak," he tells me. "We have a long journey ahead of us in order to get to Thebes today, the city I mentioned. Especially if you wish to have edible food instead of the rations we had last night. Please continue to wear your disguise. You must resemble the rest the group as much as possible. At least from a distance."

"Don't you wear the Corinthian helmet, with the faceguard, and horsehair plume on top?" I inquire.

"No, that is not worn anymore either."

"Oh."

The soldiers pack up my tent and the blankets, and we are soon on our way. I secure my basket to me with a rope. Dew is thick on the grass. The smell of rain is in the air while I notice black clouds in the distance. "Do you think it will storm?" I ask Kriton.

"Yes," he answers, as our horses trot along. "But the weather should clear up by noontime."

"How do you know that?"

He shrugs. "I know weather like you know Apollo, Lady Selene."

"That is a wonderful and sometimes terrible gift," I joke with him.

"Indeed," he declares, beaming.

I enjoy talking with Kriton. He is agreeable and smart. I am hungry, not just for food, but for intelligent and friendly dialogue as well.

"How do you come by your shrewdness?" I ask. "You are amazingly articulate and lucid."

"Thank you for noticing. Although I am a soldier of fortune, I am not a dullard. We will talk later. That direction is Delphi," he points to his left, "but for now we are riding straight ahead to Thebes. We must whip our horses into a gallop, to get as far as possible before the storm breaks." He kicks his horse in the side, and it takes off running and snorting. I follow suit as do his four *hoplite* companions.

I wrap my legs tightly around my horse's belly, trying to remain mounted, but with some difficulty.

Kriton quickly perceives my dilemma and rides back to me. "Lady Selene, when we get to Thebes, I will replace that horse with a *Pindos* pony. The *Pindos* is small, muscular and obedient. Thus it will be easier for you to ride."

"Thank you, Kriton," gritting my teeth, intending to hold on to the animal for all I'm worth.

"I have an idea, Lady. Why don't you ride with me? I'm easier to hold on to than that mare."

We stop. The Commander helps me off my mount, while a *hoplite* companion assists me to climb on behind Kriton."

I am at ease, no longer worried about falling off the tall horse, while clinging to the man in front of me.

The soldier grabs hold of the reins of the now rider-less horse and we take off again.

* * *

Late in the day as we approach Thebes, I see the city is situated in a large valley, in the middle of which is a low rocky ridge, an acropolis, similar to that of Athens, only lower and longer with a wall running around it. A lower level is situated below the wall, surrounded by yet a second wall. Streams run through the plain, crops grow in abundance, so I imagine the city must be prosperous. We are all damp and somewhat bedraggled from the earlier rain. Large herds of horses graze near the ridge.

"You see, Lady Selene?" Kriton shouts, pointing ahead of us. "Thebes is famous for its Thessalian horses, like these we ride. That wall surrounds Kadmeia, the acropolis. There are seven gates leading into the upper city."

I peer to where he is pointing. "I can see several. Are those part of the famous Seven Gates I have read about?"

"Yes. Each gate opens to a different part of Boeotia. We are heading towards the Protides Gate, which faces southeast towards Athens, the direction we have come from."

As he speaks, we notice a group approaching us on horseback from the city.

Kriton and the others quickly stop their horses. "Do not speak, Lady Selene. I know Thebans and they are mistrustful of strangers. Particularly those from Athens."

"But…"

"We will have no problems. First I must explain the situation to them."

"All right. I am in your hands."

Kriton motions to our band to remain where we are. He helps me dismount and seats me on the extra horse, then gallops over to the coming group and they converse still astride their horses, accompanied with much waving of arms and shouting. The interchange lasts for some time while I grow anxious.

"Be at peace, Lady," one of the *hoplites* from our small contingent tells me as he holds my reins. "Thebans are hot-blooded and talk loudly."

"I can see that," I comment ironically.

"Kriton was born here and grew up with these people. He will know what to say."

I wait impatiently, hoping for the best. Then I receive a short message from Apollo. "All is well and in perfect order." I relax, knowing we are safe.

Kriton rides back to us, grinning broadly. "I have explained everything to them and they agree. We may pass and enter the city. Follow me," and he gallops back in the direction of the city. At the base of the acropolis, he springs from his horse, and signals to the six of us to follow him. The group from the city has disappeared from view.

Our little band of horses trots over to Kriton. The men dismount.

"Good news, Lady Selene! We are invited to stay with the Governor of Thebes and his family tonight. They are hurrying to prepare a banquet in your honor."

"My honor? I am confused. One moment I am a fugitive. The next I am being feted at a banquet?"

"Lady Selene, daughter of Delphi, you are famous! When you were living in Naxos, the Governor of Thebes attended a reading hosted by your husband in which you read for a number of people. Governor Gorgias was one of those who received a reading."

He helps me down from the horse.

Kriton is cackling loudly. "A banquet, Lady Selene. For you. You will eat well tonight—unlike yesterday!"

The horses are sent out to graze in a fenced pasture. "My basket," I cry out. Kriton rescues the reed basket containing coins, scrolls, the bee necklace, and my precious figurine. I resolutely carry the basket, hugging it close to me.

The seven of us are met by an official, and we climb up steep stone steps to the Governor's manse. The house is amazingly built into the rocks of the cliff—a feat of architecture and a. fortress besides.

Governor Gorgias himself greets us at the massively hinged open wooden door. "Lady Selene of Delphi. Welcome! I am privileged to have you grace my humble abode." He turns to an exquisitely dressed woman, sparkling with jewelry, standing next to him. "Wife, this is the extraordinary woman I told you about when I was at Naxos last year. Lady Selene. This is my wife, Charmion."

Kriton and the other four men stand silently as they watch the remarkable proceedings.

Charmion bows. "It is my pleasure to celebrate you in my husband's home," she murmurs graciously. She observes my clothing and a look of hesitancy comes over her features, but she is too well-bred to say anything.

I am horrified as I realize how I must appear. Wearing filthy clothes, wet from rain, ineptly disguised as a *hoplite* soldier, my hair clumsily tucked into a helmet, and smelling like a sweaty horse.

"Let me find you something suitable to wear, Lady Selene," she says diplomatically, and leads me to her private chamber.

Kriton watches, trying to disguise a smirk.

"We have a bathing compartment you may use to wash up," she adds.

"Thank you for your utmost kindness."

"Your being here is a rare privilege. It is not every day that we entertain a Delphic Oracle."

I will have to straighten out their confusion. Later. After dinner.

Hardly containing my giggles, I wash and dress with the help of Charmion's personal slave. If Demetria were here to know what has transpired, she would be amused as well. As an Athenian, I am an enemy of Sparta, but celebrated and feted by a Spartan ally. I am rescued from my husband by a soldier in broad daylight in the marketplace in Athens. I hide in the wilds of Boeotia, while fighting goes on around us then gallop wildly to Thebes with a band of mercenary *hoplite* warriors, dressed as one of them. Finally the Governor's wife bows to me in homage while I wear disgustingly dirty, smelly clothes.

This scenario could be a comedy written by a new playwright named Aristophanes.

* * *

I arrive in the dining hall dressed in one of Madame Charmion's many chitons, with a delicate *chlamys* over it, finished by a veil with gold flecks in it. My hair is coiffed in aristocratic Theban style as only a slave with artistic genius can accomplish. I attempt to talk to the slave, but she shakes her head and points to her mouth. She is mute.

"Lady Selene. You are beautiful as well as gifted," the Governor's wife says to me courteously when I arrive, and seats me between herself and her husband. "Peach is a color well suited to your golden hair, fair skin, and blue eyes," she comments with appreciation.

"I must apologize again for showing up at your elegant home dressed as a beggar or a soldier. Or both."

She titters. "Kriton explained to my husband of your narrow escape. I find it entertaining."

What has Kriton told the Governor? He knows the value of a good story told well. With Kriton's clever words and shrewd mind my narrative grew and became embellished. How did such a man become a soldier? I would like to hear that tale.

The food is delicious and well-prepared. I have had little food in three days, so I eat until I am fit to burst yet the Governor and his wife encourage me to try other dishes arriving periodically from the kitchen. "You do me great honor," I say. "But I cannot eat one more morsel. I offer my appreciation to the cook for a delightful meal."

Governor Gorgias acknowledges my words. "Our cook is from the island of Krete. She is a distant ancestor of the Minoans who lived there long ago. I found her and her culinary skills during my travels, purchased her from her owner at a prohibitive cost, and relocated her here."

"She is a treasure," Madame Charmion adds.

I notice that they do not mention the cook's name. The woman is merely a slave. With an indispensable skill of preparing delectable food. Like the slave who can dress hair. I become ill at ease. Would having an essential skill apply to me as well? Are they grooming me to be another slave, one able to call on Apollo?

Kriton and the other *hoplites* are dining in a different room. I can hear their uproarious conversation and joking emanating through the hallway. They must have been served wine.

The Governor rises to his feet, a nonverbal message for banqueters to retire. He motions to me to remain. All others leave with appropriate well wishes for a good night's rest.

Kriton and the *hoplite* soldiers remain in the small dining room. The adjoining door has been shut and sounds are now muted.

Once the others have departed he sits and begins speaking. "Lady Selene."

"Yes, my lord," I reply.

"You are an extremely gifted woman."

"Thank you, Governor."

"Do you remember what you told me at Naxos at the reading from Apollo?"

"No, your grace. I do not. But that is not unusual. Often there are too many guests for me to remember details."

"Nevertheless," he waves his hand imperiously. "You told me that my son would soon wed a woman who would bring me much good fortune. Power. Money. Connections. You described her to the last detail." He paused for emphasis. "My son Gennadius did just that. He married Timothea, daughter of a Spartan King. During the wedding banquet, her father King Pleistoanax took me aside and asked if I would sign an exclusive military pact between Thebes and Sparta. I did so on the spot because of what you, I mean Apollo, told me. Everything that was revealed during the reading is coming to pass. I have become wealthy and powerful, while my son will inherit it all when I die. I owe an enormous debt to you, Lady Selene."

"I don't know what to say, Honorable Gorgias. I am thrilled that all has worked out well for you."

"Lady Selene. Remain with me. Stay here in Thebes. Continue your work. You can help many other people, as you have helped me and my family."

"Governor. Your kind offer is splendid. I would be a fool to say no. But, sir, I must say no. I am on a mission of my own, which must be completed."

"Whatever you ask for, Lady Selene, it will be done. I can help you with your mission, too, if you like." His tone turns menacing. "Just do not leave."

"May we talk about this tomorrow?" I delay, more apprehensive than before. "I am weary from the long trip."

"Of course. I have a room ready for you. I have lodged your *hoplite* rescuers as well. They will receive a reward for liberating you and bringing you here to Thebes, to my house. They tell me you need a *Pindos* pony to ride. I have arranged one for you as my gift. It is yours for journeying around Thebes."

"That is gratifying. The soldiers assisted me tremendously. Good night, honorable sir." I stand, anxious to exit the hall.

"Good night, darling Selene." He suddenly positions himself in front of me, reaches unceremoniously to clutch my shoulder. Then he kisses me on the lips, while thrusting his tongue into my mouth in an obscene and lascivious manner.

I jerk away from his embrace as though a wasp has stung me. This powerful man, the Governor, is not to be trusted.

"I will call a slave to show you to your chamber," he informs me, his eyes glowing with desire and greed.

When I arrive at the room, shaking with apprehension, I bolt the door. I sleep not at all.

Chapter 18

KALAMBAKA   AGE 28   422 BC

10th year of the war. An official truce is sustained until late summer, yet fighting continues.

* * *

I am up at dawn to seek out Kriton, wary of the Governor and his plans for me.

Kriton and the other *hoplites* are outside, all of whom are recovering from the night before. They are eating some freshly baked pita bread served with thick yogurt and some grapes.

"Lady Selene," he shouts and waves.

I hurry over to him.

"Did you have a favorable talk with the Governor?"

"Kriton. We cannot stay here," I announce breathlessly.

"I thought the two of you were getting along well. Your fame preceded you and he was delighted to have such an illustrious guest." His eyes are bloodshot from last night's wine.

"I am serious, Kriton," with exasperation. "If I stay here, I will become a prisoner. One more slave in his harem of talented women."

"What transpires between you and men, Lady Selene?" he asks jokingly.

"It is not me. It is the sickness of our society," I try to explain. I describe Gorgias' behavior and demeanor of the night before.

"I sympathize, Lady Selene. Women are thought of as property. A man can take what he wants. Do what he wants, to whatever woman he wants, with license."

"Yes, that is what I mean. The Governor is used to having his way in all matters. He means to exploit me to further his ambitions. Perhaps other preoccupations as well." I grimace, wanting to erase the brief encounter from my mind.

"I am not like that, Lady Selene," he responds with sincerity, all teasing now put aside.

"I hope not," I respond vehemently. "I am counting on you, Kriton. Meanwhile I must get a clean *chiton* to wear and collect my basket. We need to depart as soon as possible."

"The Governor will be greatly offended when you leave." Kriton ponders for a moment. "I have known him for a few years. Gorgias is an astute politician and military strategist, although I've never seen him mistreat a woman. But once his ire is aroused...."

"You are not a woman, so you could not recognize his behavior," I interrupt. "He is subtle but his actions and intentions are clear. I'm certain much goes on behind closed doors."

"I believe you." He adds, "They gave back the red *chlamys* and the helmet because they thought you weren't leaving with us."

"I will need them. Let us make arrangements quickly and leave. The Governor gave me a *Pindos* pony," I add.

"Yes, I have learned that. We shall take her as well. She will be much easier for you to ride. We have packed the extra horse and will take her with us as well."

Within minutes, I am dressed in a plain linen *chiton*, with new sandals on my feet, donated by the mute slave, and have my basket with its precious contents in hand. Kriton and the other soldiers have watered and fed the animals. We are ready to ride. He hands me the red *chlamys*, which is soiled and smelly but intact, and the helmet, both of which I put on, pushing my un-coiffed hair inside the *Pilos*.

"I obtained food from the cook." I show him the basket, edibles wrapped in cloth.

"Good planning." He face becomes woeful. "I'm very sorry, Lady Selene. This is my fault."

"No one is at fault, Kriton. Please, let us hurry away from this awful place!"

The six of us gallop off heading north. No one of importance in the fortress is the wiser for the time being. They are sleeping off last night's banquet.

"I won't feel at peace until we are far from Thebes." I can feel Apollo's soothing touch. "Apollo tells me we will be safe," I shout.

Kriton waves in response.

Holding tightly to the reins, my legs wrapped around the pony's middle, I feverishly ride. I never look back, afraid that the demons of Hades, the Lamiai, under the auspices of Hekate, are chasing us.

At the height of the day, exhausted, we stop at a shady spot with a stream running through it.

"The horses need to rest and drink," one of the *hoplites* mention, "while we need water and food ourselves. This is a good place to take a break from our arduous journey."

"Thank you, soldier," I commend him, going through the basket to find our food. Then I remove the *Pilos* helmet, shaking my hair loose. "What is your name?"

"Cosmos, Revered Mistress," he replies.

"Thank you for your help, Cosmos."

"It is my duty," he says to me with respect then adds, "I had no idea you are such an exalted personage."

I laugh. "I am not exalted, but have a task to do, as you yourself have."

Kriton has been listening to our conversation. "Lady Selene is unique," he mentions to Cosmos.

The *hoplite* nods and goes to check his horse, while munching on a piece of cold cooked chicken from the Governor's kitchen.

"Your demeanor and loveliness affect others, Lady Selene," he declares, watching Cosmos as he leaves.

"I must look outlandish," restraining a giggle. "I do the best I can, Kriton."

"I believe that, Lady. We must get far away from Thebes. There are wild places north of here in Thessaly below Macedonia, where we can disappear."

After we have eaten, I am helped to mount my pony, and we gallop towards Thessaly.

* * *

Our group spends many months evading capture. As predicted, Apollo informs me that Gorgias is infuriated and commands my return, especially having taken the valuable pony with me. However, the god is always one step ahead of Gorgias and his men. Thus we are safely hidden and practically invisible. Apollo also advises us where fighting is occurring so we can avoid those areas, too.

Kriton and his men know the country well. In addition to their long spears and daggers, they have bows and arrows with them to catch wild game to cook over the campfire. Periodically we find a small village or hamlet where we rest and obtain food.

"My money is useful."

"Keep your coins," he advises me. "There are other ways of obtaining what we need." Often Kriton charms people into giving away food, equipment, clothing, and blankets or else trading services for what we need. He and his fellow *hoplites* have many skills for hire.

Once in a while, in a larger town, we have an inn to sleep in, with a real, although thin, mattress. Otherwise we slumber on the hard ground, under the stars, in our well-worn tents while my body aches relentlessly.

As we travel, strangers look at us with a mixture of curiosity and confusion, especially at me. Of the six of us, I stand out, especially wearing the red *chlamys* and helmet. Perhaps some people consider me to be a camp follower and dismiss me as such.

There is no one to pass on Apollo's messages in these remote places, nor do I want to be recognized. Doing public readings would only alert Gorgias to our whereabouts.

We travel on to Thessaly.

"Winter is coming and we will need a warm place to stay," Kriton tells me. "You must delay your mission until spring."

We stop at a spring bubbling out of the ground. The animals are watered and have some shrubbery to eat, while we rest and eat whatever is left of our traveling food we procured along the way.

"Are we close to our next destination? I long for a place to sleep off the hard ground, somewhere we don't have to hide and pretend, but can remain for a while."

Kriton explains. "Kalambaka is the perfect place. We will soon pass Mt. Pelion and Mt. Ossa to the east. These are coastal ranges of Ossa and Pelion that border the sea. Mt. Olympus, sacred home of the gods, is far to the northwest, part of the Olympos chain of mountains."

"The mountains are lovely. They remind me of Mt. Parnassus."

"Families have lived here since extremely ancient times, becoming wealthy and powerful, due to the richness of the lowlands from various tributaries of the Pineios River." He continues, "We will overwinter in Kalambaka in the river valley. Many pilgrims travel to that town because of the nearness of Mt. Olympus as well as a place called Meteora."

"What is that?"

"Meteora is an unusual location. An expanse of cliffs rises vertically from a flat plain towards the sky. There is no way to get to the tops of any of them unless you can fly like an eagle. The rock outcroppings are exquisite to see and inspiring. You might even say magical."

"We must go!" I exclaim.

"In the early spring we can travel to Meteora. We will be able to see Olympus silhouetted against the rock formations. I was there once, long ago."

"Sounds heavenly," I breathe.

* * *

When we arrive at Kalambaka, Kriton guides us to an inn at the edge of the town.

"Stay here with the men, Lady Selene. I will inquire about rooms."

"Do you need money?" I ask, indicating my basket.

"Let me see what can be arranged."

After a time, Cosmos approaches me shyly. "Lady Selene?"

"Yes, Cosmos."

"You will be able to rest here," he speaks kindly.

"I hope so."

"We are all weary."

Just then Kriton returns. "I have obtained two rooms for us until spring. A little room for you, Lady Selene, with a small bed with a thick mattress. Also a large one, where the five of us will camp on the floor. There is a *taverna* on the premises where they serve food. The owner advises me that various women of the village often cook for guests staying at the inn."

Cosmos shouts in triumph. "Cooked food!"

"Thank you, Kriton," I tell him. "How much will it cost?"

"No money is required," he murmurs. "The lads and I will work in exchange for the rooms. It is all arranged."

"I cannot let you…"

"The labor is of no concern, Lady Selene. We are strong and used to it. This has been our way of life for years." He smiles warmly at me. "Thank you for your kind interest. Pray, let us continue to care for you while we are able."

"You are a worthy man, Kriton."

"You have a home for now, Lady Selene," and he leads the way to my room, not simply out of courtesy but also to protect me. I have my basket gripped in my hand. He leaves, encouraging me to slide the bolt shut behind him. A small cracked stone basin stands on a small table, with a jar of water at its side. I pour the water into the basin, wash my face and hands and wipe them on a cloth provided. The room is meager but clean.

The men lead the horses and pony to a small fenced area. After they have moved the tents, blankets, weapons, and clothing the large room, we regroup in the *taverna*. The tantalizing aroma of cooking meat permeates the space.

The owner's skinny son comes over to the table. The boy looks oddly at me but does not comment. "Goat stew tonight," he declares.

"Could we have bread with that?'" Cosmos asks.

"Yes."

Kriton signals to me to remain silent, then orders goat stew with bread for all of us. "I would like some watered wine if you have it," he tells the boy.

"All we have is retsina," the young man explains.

"That is fine. Please bring a pitcher of water as well."

The stew, as is usual for goat, is filled with small bones, so we eat carefully.

After dinner the men are drained and return to their large room, while Kriton escorts me to mine.

Although I'm fatigued, I would rather talk with Kriton than sleep.

"I miss our talks," Kriton says touchingly when we arrive at my door.

"I do, too."

"Then let us go to the *taverna*," and he leads the way. A fire has been lit in the hearth and the room is toasty warm on this frigid autumn night, unoccupied except for the two of us.

We sit together on a wooden bench at a table, next to each other, suddenly awkward.

I pull the well-worn red *chlamys* tightly around my shoulders. "It is invaluable that you know of this town and the inn."

"Yes, it is," he agrees. "I have been here before, years ago." He seems troubled. "Have you received messages from Apollo lately?"

"No. I ignore anything having to do with war, so little is left to hear."

"Can you do that?"

"Do what?"

"Ignore Apollo."

"It is like disregarding the sounds of the horses as they race across the plain. The sounds become background noises and I concentrate on what is in front of me instead. Do you understand?"

"Not really," he chuckles with candor.

"Hmmm," and I smile with delight. "I haven't heard you laugh for days."

"I have been thinking."

"Thinking about what?"

"About what I will do when our arrangement is finished and you return to Delphi," he speaks frankly.

"I need to finish my task before I can go home."

"Yes, I understand. What precisely is your task, Lady Selene?"

"To find someone."

"Do you know where that someone is living?"

"Not exactly. Twice Apollo sent me messages. I see bluffs overlooking the sea. A small group of houses. Laundry spread out on grass."

"That could be anywhere."

"Yes, but I feel I am close since coming to this town."

"Perhaps in the spring? It is getting too cold to travel."

"Yes."

Kriton changes the awkward subject. "Do you know that Cadmus of Thebes introduced writing to Greece? Thebans are an educated people."

"Mmm hmm," I reply. "Except for Governor Gorgias who is a vulgar man."

"Not counting him," Kriton agrees laughing.

"However, being educated is certainly true of you. I sometimes wonder how you know so much."

"I was a military diplomat for the current Governor and the one before him as well. I started when I was 15. My father taught me all he knew, as well as some reading and writing, which no one else studied. He believed I was smart and quick. I questioned everything and thereby gleaned answers." He chuckles. "My questioning must have annoyed him but he never told me to stop. I am curious about many subjects. I find myself becoming easily bored, so the life of a soldier, a mercenary, suits me."

"Do I bore you?"

"Never!" he replies without hesitation. "In fact, I wish there was a door to your head, which I could open, so I could to discover information you have stored in there."

"That is why I like scrolls. As if many people's heads are pouring forth knowledge while I simply sit and read. Those people's words are always available. Unlike real people, they never get tired, so I can read the texts any time."

"You offered once to read to me from one of your scrolls. Could you do that now?"

"Yes, if you would like." I look around. "The light is too dim to read in here. We could get together sometime during the day. When you don't have work to do." I flush. "I am ill at ease that you and your men will toil while I will sit around all day."

"Then write, Lady Selene," he suggests. "Your words are precious."

"I am flattered that you think so."

"I will find some writing materials so that you can express what lives in your head, including messages from Apollo."

"Writing will be my work."

He hesitates. "I have a question that has puzzled me."

"Yes?"

"Why does Apollo give messages to both Athenians and Peloponnesians? They are enemies."

"Apollo doesn't take sides. I don't either."

The portly owner comes up to us. "The *taverna* is closed now. It will be open again in the morning."

"Thank you for letting us know," Kriton replies civilly. "We will retire to our chambers now." He escorts me to my door. "Always a pleasure, Lady Selene."

"Good night, Kriton."

* * *

Thus I spend time writing as if I am a scribe, while Kriton and the other *hoplites* work like slaves. After I finish each scroll that I have written upon, I wrap it carefully in oiled goat skin to protect it.

Winter comes and goes. Bare trees begin to leaf. Ewes give birth. A huge celebration takes place in Kalambaka. To celebrate Persephone's return from the underworld the villagers butcher and cook many young lambs. They invite us to eat roasted lamb along with watered wine during the daylong festivities.

Crocus are blooming. Soon narcissus will flower along with daffodils. Olives will be pressed into oil. Winter onions are being harvested. Chickens will soon be laying eggs again as there is more light in the lengthening days while the sun continues its yearly journey towards the summer solstice.

With the return of spring, Apollo's messages to find Heraclius become insistent.

"Kriton, it is time for us to leave. The person I am looking for lives in a small village on the coast of the sea. We are close."

"Lady Selene. As always, I am at your disposal."

"I'm sorry there will be no time for you to show me Meteora. I would have liked to see the rock formations."

"There is no problem." He adds, "I understand the urgency."

Chapter 19

Milossa and Corinne   age 29   421 BC

Before we leave Kalambaka news of the war arrives from messengers on horseback. The Peace of Nicias has been declared between Athens and Sparta, although fighting continues occasionally.

Simonides writes commemorating the end of battle:
"Rest at ease, my long lance, against the tall column
sacred to Panomphaean Zeus;
your point is now dull from age, and you're scorched,
brandished in one war after another."

The vision of Heraclius appears every morning, spurring me on. We journey, stopping at every village and hamlet near the Aegean, to determine if he lives there. There are no inns outside cities, which we mostly avoid anyway. We travel through the Spercheious Valley, which is walled in by large mountains on three sides—the Pindus, the Ossa, and Othrys—while the eastern part faces the sea with its sandy beaches. The valley is home to horse breeding and grain farming. Kriton informs me that, to the north, Dion is a large metropolis in the region of Pieria, the northeastern part of Greece.

We continue our journey east towards the Aegean.

When we arrive in Milossa my feelings and messages are over-whelming. I sense I have arrived at my long sought-after destination. The village of Milossa consists of several dozen ramshackle cottages on a bluff overlooking the sea, a day's ride from Dion. I can't imagine Heraclius living here.

With help from Kriton I dismount, encouraging the pony to eat the fresh greenery growing near the bluff. I turn to Kriton. "Can you and the men allow us to talk privately? Over there perhaps?" I point to a grassy hillock.

"Yes, Lady Selene. We will do that." He gives the order and they walk their horses in that direction, while he grasps the pony's reins in his hand.

I saunter a few paces, heading to the nearest hut. Before I arrive, I spy a young, discernibly pregnant woman, accompanied by two small children, spreading laundry on the ground to dry in the hot sun.

"Hello, Lady," I hail the young woman. "I am sorry to disturb you. I am looking for a man named Heraclius," I tell her.

She barely looks up, busy with her work. "There is no one in our village by that name."

"Are you certain?" I question her.

"Yes, absolutely." She straightens up and pushes a few wisps of brown hair out of her face. She is without guile and I believe her.

"My name is Selene of Delphi. I have traveled throughout Greece to find the individual I speak of."

"I am pleased to meet you, Selene. My name is Corinne. These are my children." She indicates the two of them and regards me pleasantly.

"Those are Kriton and his troops," I point. "We have been in-formed that the war is over and peace has been established. The *hoplites* are accompanying me on my exploration, but will have to return home soon."

Corinne holds up her hand, shielding her eyes from the bright sunlight. "Oh," she replies with little interest. Her laundry has more appeal than my story.

"You have beautiful children," I comment.

"Thank you," she replies in appreciation, now more attentive.

"How old are they?"

My son is three years old and the girl almost two. I am expecting another one soon."

"The gods be with you and your wonderful family." Then I summon courage to remark candidly. "Your son seems big for three years old."

"Oh, yes," she continues. "My husband is extremely tall and our son takes after him," she says proudly.

My hair stands on end and truth bumps rise on my arms, while the hair on the back of my neck stands up. "What is your husband's name?"

"Alex," she says. "There he is now," and she waves at her husband approaching us.

I hold my breath as Corinne's husband walks our way. The man has an athletic body, with long arms and legs. As he nears, I see he has a jagged scar running from his forehead through his left eye down to his cheek. Without it he might have been handsome.

"Husband," Corinne takes his arm. "We have visitors. This is Selene. I forget the soldier's name over there."

"Go to the house, Corinne, and take the children," the man commands imperiously, shaking off her hand.

"Why Alex? Is something wrong?"

"You know I don't like you talking to strangers," he continues. "In wartime no one is safe."

"But Selene has informed me that the war has ended."

"Has it?" the man asks with surprise. "Corinne. Do what I say. I need to talk to these… strangers. I have questions I must ask."

"Yes, husband. I will do as you command." Corinne takes the two children by their small hands and returns to their simple home, period-ically looking back at us with curiosity as she does so.

"Selene. Is it really you?" he questions me quietly when the young woman is out of earshot.

"Heraclius? I hardly recognize you. Your face…"

He raises his hand to hide the unsightly scar. "I cannot talk to you for long. Then you must leave and never return."

"I don't understand, Heraclius."

"No one has called me that in a long time. My name is Alex now. I must talk quickly."

"All right," I tentatively agree.

"Please do not judge me for what I am about to say."

"Why would I judge you?"

He interrupts. "During the first year of the war, I prepared for bat-tle against the enemy with my *hoplite* companions. We were protecting the fort at Oenoe. We grouped outside to fight Peloponnesians, to de-fend the fortress."

Scrolls are deeply imbedded in my mind. Even at this delicate mo-ment I remember Aeschylus:

"Not in retreat were the Greek soldiers singing
The sacred battle-hymn, no, they were rushing
To combat, hopeful, even confident.
Their hearts took fire from a bellowing trumpet…"

Heraclius appears quite overwrought and struggles to continue. "We formed the phalanx as I once described to you."

I nod.

"We stood as one, shields linked together through many rows, as a single unit, waiting for the enemy to come near, so that we could attack en masse. I had my javelin in one hand, shield in the other, and a dagger in my belt." He pauses and wipes his sweaty face.

I can barely breathe, listening to his litany.

"The enemy employed cavalry rather than ground troops. I could hear their horses' hooves pounding the ground, rushing towards us. This was not the athletic games, Selene, as I participated in for years, merely playing at war. The challenge before me was life or death." He pauses in remembrance.

"Please continue."

"I broke ranks. I shattered the phalanx, and ran away. The most dishonorable action a warrior can take. I left my comrades to fend for themselves, while I ran like a coward towards some nearby trees to hide myself." He confesses his actions to me with shame.

I am gripped by his story.

"While I hid, I watched the entire company of my comrades viciously massacred by the Spartan cavalry. No man was left alive. Only I survived."

I gasp.

"But then I saw an enemy horseman wheel his horse and veer towards me. He had his long spear in his hand, heading in my direction. I froze, not knowing what to do or where to run. His horse charged and at the last moment he threw the spear towards me. With the force of the running horse, his spear struck my helmet. I felt the tip of his spear hit. Fortunately I was wearing a Corinthian helmet, not the *Pilos* that had become popular, or I might have been killed instantly."

"Oh gods!" I exclaim.

"I fell to the ground unconscious while he galloped away, perhaps thinking he had killed me. When I awoke, dried blood covered my face. I couldn't see out of my left eye. There was no way I could return to my countrymen, Selene. My *arête*, my victorious valor, was smashed along with my head. I had dishonored myself, Aegeus, and all of Athens. There was no choice but to run away. Somewhere that no one knew me, or my name. I was as good as dead."

I groan.

"The enemy had departed. My helmet lay cracked on the ground. I removed my armor and hid it under some leaves in the forest, now dressed only in my *chiton*. I followed the line of trees until I came to a meadow. I walked for days until I found a village. A kind old woman patched me up and nursed me until my terrible injury healed, and fortunately asked no questions. But I was completely blind in my left eye. I departed before they could discover my identity. I made my way here to Milossa, where I could start life anew without fear of recognition."

Heraclius is not the jovial man I used to know, but a deeply injured soul. "Why didn't you contact me or Aegeus? Return to Athens?"

"You don't appreciate my situation, Selene."

"I understand that you deserted your loved ones. We waited for years to find you. Thinking you might be dead, but hoping you were alive."

"I was dead. I am dead."

"I have been searching, Heraclius. I attached myself to that group of *hoplite* soldiers over there in my hunt for you. I traveled throughout much of Greece, trying to find you."

"Oh, dear Selene. I am so sorry."

"We have a son, Heraclius!" My voice becomes shrill with emotion.

"A son," he repeats incredulously.

"His name is Tydeus!" I become overwhelmed saying the boy's name out loud. Years of longing and misery arise at the mention of our son's name. "He is in Athens where I abandoned him. So that I could find his father."

"You must never tell Tydeus about me, Selene. I couldn't bear it. Don't be angry with me."

I'm not angry at you!" I shout, pulling myself as tall as I could as I spoke, although far shorter than him. "I'm enraged. Furious. Terrible as the gorgon sister Medusa, with snakes hissing round my head, ready to consume your loins. Fiery as Thera when it erupted, washing away the precious Minoan world. Leaving the rest of the world with.... what? War? Battle? Honor? I spit on your honor."

He glares at me.

"You ran away from battle. There is no honor in that. When you buried your armor in the forest, your buried your family, along with responsibilities, fatherhood, and husbandhood. Then you entomb yourself in this forsaken place. Seduce a wife. Sperm a family into being. Attempt to become a different man. But one thing you fail to understand. You are the same man, cowardly and despicable to everyone who has ever known you. You are not a warrior. You are a frightened, timid, shell of a man who turned his back on everything and everyone you knew, those who love you."

Heraclius starts to speak, but I stop him with an upheld hand facing towards him. I scowl in a terrifying grimace. "I cannot force you to come home with me. You are married and hide behind the mantle of Corinne. Why should I help you break the heart of another woman and desert more children? But I can fracture your name into a thousand shards of disgrace when I return to Delphi, even as far away as Athens. I assure you that is exactly what I intend to do."

"You lie. What you say is unfair and untrue." He refutes my statements.

"No, I do not lie. But your disrepute will follow you like a shadow throughout the rest of your life and into the waiting arms of Hades, also known as Pluton, in the underworld."

He blanches at the vision, beads of sweat beginning to drip down his brow. His scarred face is twisted in poignant agony. "I've always loved you."

I continue without pause. My fury has taken on a life of its own and I cannot stop. "You never loved anyone. You used all of us because you could and wanted to do so. Every act is based on your own selfish desires, without regard to anyone. Arrogance and lust have been your faithful companions."

"Grant me forgiveness," he pleads.

I continue unabated, without compassion. "When you arrive in the underworld you will be greeted by Cerberus, growling and clawing at your old, shriveled body, unlike the one you still have today. Mark my words. Care for that body as you will. Your physical being cannot last forever, but my story will."

"Selene!" he cries pitiably, falling to his knees in misery.

Without another word I turn and sprint over to the waiting group of *hoplites*. I am livid and shaking with anger. "Kriton, let us be gone and return to Delphi! I was mistaken. There is nothing here worth saving. My long search has been in vain."

"Lady Selene. I will see you back to Delphi safely, though a season may come and go before we arrive." He takes my trembling hand and leads me to my waiting pony, helping me to mount.

As we ride off, I turn to glance back. Heraclius is kneeling in the field, a devastated man. That image is branded into my mind for eternity. For the moment, though, anger keeps me from lamenting.

After we have ridden far from Milossa, Kriton gallops up next to me. "Lady Selene, do you see any problems waiting for us on the trail home?"

"What?" I inquire, yanking on the reins to stop the pony, while he does the same with his horse. "I'm sorry, Kriton. I have been thinking about matters not related to our trip home."

"Many pardons, Lady. I am concerned about any skirmishes we may encounter." Although outwardly he seems casually curious, he is scrutinizing me intently.

"We are safe. No one and nothing will bother us during our long trek back to Delphi. The war is over. I hope the peace will be lasting."

"That is surely good news. Thank you for your ever-truthful visions."

"My pleasure as always. Thank you for caring for me during… " My voice breaks.

"Lady Selene?" Kriton inquires. He dismounts his horse and takes hold of my pony's mane. He is clearly troubled and self-conscious. I have never seen him thus with either friend or foe.

"What is the matter?" I ask Kriton.

"You were looking for a man during the entire time you have been with us." It is a statement rather than a question.

"Yes," I say simply. "You have known that."

"Yes, I have, since the beginning. You have been honorable in your quest and unflinching in your search."

"I tried to be."

"Was that disgraceful thing the man you were looking for?" He nods indignantly towards the village indicating Heraclius.

"Yes," I answer wretchedly. "That is the man. My search is over."

"You did not find who you were hoping for?" He examines my eyes, hopeful.

"The person I wanted to locate does not exist. He is dead." I shut my eyes but a few stray tears betray me.

"Lady Selene. Honored Priestess." He hesitates. "Dear one."

"What?" I am startled by his change in tone. I have never heard him address me in this intimate manner before now.

"Forgive me. I have no right to speak to you like this," as he continues to hold the reins in his strong, leathery hand. "You… we have been on this path a long time. You have counseled me and my *hoplites* with grace, honor, dignity, and truth. With as much valor, *arête*, as a warrior. You have warned us of danger. You have advised us how to proceed. You have kept us safe."

I nod my head. I am suddenly so fatigued I fear I might fall, and attempt to steady myself.

He continues. "I have esteemed you all this time."

"Kriton. What do you say? Is this seemly?" I am taken by surprise. Or is it a surprise? Did I recognize his feelings long ago and pretended not to see? How could an Oracle not know her future?

"No, perhaps not, Selene. But it is my truth as I discern it. Have I ever treated you badly? With *hybris* or offense? With unwarranted behavior or words?"

"No, never. Not once."

"Then let me tell you this now while I have courage. Eros shot me in my simple aging warrior heart after rescuing you in the Agora that day. I am not a scholar like you. I am not handsome. Nor am I rich and powerful. I am a battered old soldier and will soon turn 40. But I declare to you that I wish to marry you and care for you in the manner you deserve, wherever you want to live. If you will have me."

Kriton's proposal is extraordinary, not usually expressed from a man to a woman, but rather arranged through families. However, there is no family to speak for me. I am not an ordinary woman. This is not a conventional situation.

I cannot bear to look down at his kind face filled with admiration and affection. "Help me to get down, Kriton," and he does so.

I stand next to him. "With your words and demeanor you are showing me great honor. Perhaps the greatest honor I could be gifted with. You are a good man, Kriton. A worthy man. But..." I pause.

"But?"

"I must return to Delphi. To determine if my mother still lives and for her to know that I am alive as well. I have been gone a long time and news doesn't travel well during war. Apollo has never illuminated her fate to me."

"My pleasure will be to escort you there."

"Peace has finally come to Greece, Kriton. We can return without worry." I look deeply into his dependable eyes, summoning nerve to expose my secret. He deserves my honesty. I take a deep breath and continue. "I have a husband and a child in Athens. I do not know if they are alive or dead."

"I know about the husband. You have a child as well?"

I continue quickly, disgrace reddening my face. "Yes, I deserted him to go on this pursuit, when you rescued me that day in Athens. It was wicked of me. But I had no choice. My husband's name is Aegeus and my son is Tydeus."

"I see." Kriton looks down at his worn, dusty sandals, not knowing what else to say. "Regardless, I wish to wed you," he murmurs quietly, then resolutely looks into my eyes. "Who do I need to ask for permission? Is there an arrangement to be made, money to be paid, to release you from former vows? I can raise your son…"

"That seems unlikely." I shrug my shoulders. "Aegeus adopted Tydeus legally. Perhaps he would let me go, but not my son. He is a possessive, obstinate man."

"That would be difficult," he agrees.

"Kriton. You deserve a woman without such a tangled history as me. A woman who has not been an Oracle. Who cannot know the future and does not live in the past. A simple woman who would love you honestly and plainly. I don't think I am that woman."

"Ah," he replies with a catch in his voice. "You do not care for me then?"

"Until today my heart was full of that other man. The unfaithful man. Disloyal to me and our son. To the army and to Athens. I need to mourn. To forget him if I am able."

"Perhaps your heart could fill once again—with love for someone else?"

"I'm not sure I can do so."

He clears his throat in embarrassment. His men are watching us and muttering to each other. He lowers his voice. "I would be honored if you would care for me as I do you. I love you, Selene. As is honorable.

I cannot imagine what misery you have endured to arrive at this place and this day. You do not seem wicked to me. You have a woman's tender heart...."

"Tender? My heart has become tough as a *hoplite*'s spear! I gathered a man's strength so that I could deliver horrifying and bloody messages from Apollo. I have arrogance, *hybris* you might call it, because I was raised to be a Delphic Oracle. The greatest honor a Greek woman could ever have." I startle him and myself with my vehemence. "I'm sorry, Kriton. I have held back feelings for years, since I was a girl. I do not mean to insult you."

"Say no more," he insists. "Let us go now. If you change your mind when we get to Delphi, let me know. I will not press you further for the moment. You are overwrought. I understand." He turns to his troops. "Let us ride while there is still light," he shouts. Then he helps me mount and hands me the reins while we ride to the southwest in brooding silence.

I whisper softly to Apollo. "Kriton is an honorable man. He would make a good husband, I think. I don't know what to do. Perhaps my sight will be clearer when we get to Delphi. I also must deal with Aegeus." A stiff wind whips at my back as the day lengthens into evening, nudging me back to Delphi.

My heart feels surprisingly heavy with Heraclius, even though I have cursed and insulted him. How can I love such a scoundrel? I must forgive him and myself. The gods have already punished him. I do not need to punish him further nor broadcast malicious words about him.

I perceive an ominous feeling, one I know well from hundreds or even thousands of readings.

"Apollo? Have I lost everything? Heraclius. My husband Aegeus. Son Tydeus. Xanthippe. Kriton. My future? Now I know what pilgrims experience when they visit the Oracle at Delphi. Hope, fear, dread, not knowing if they will receive good news or bad. A lottery of possibilities.

Waiting for your voice to shed light after an arduous journey. Impatient for information."

I straighten my back, ready for whatever eventualities would manifest for me at Delphi. The old path is finished.

It would take us a few turns of the moon to return to Delphi and the temple complex I had known intimately, played in as a child. I didn't realize it was sacred then. What is sacred anyway? I'm not sure I know. However, I realize that people want answers and Delphi provides them. Not always well-defined but valuable enough, even when answers are not wishes.

Chapter 20

SELENE'S FAMILY   AGE 30   420 BC

Battles and skirmishes continue throughout Greece.

* * *

Everything changes.

* * *

The road back to Delphi seems endless. So much has happened. Many bitter trails winding back on themselves like an infinity sign—the figure 8. Pointless war and bloodshed that I have been privy to and had to share with those in authority.

Why was it when I was a young girl hours crept slowly by? A day was a lifetime. Now every day sprints past in a blur. I can't keep up, hardly remembering what I did yesterday.

The world of people and events is confusing and complicated. Perhaps I would have been better as a simple village woman at Delphi, as I had desired. Without Apollo's gift. Without Heraclius or Aegeus, eschewing passion, fame, wealth, and honor—for peace.

Is Delphi a chimera? What would I find there? Would I continue to be a Seer? Would I be alone?

Loneliness is the worst of all possibilities, worse than deceit, trickery, lies, and even war. My life has consisted of searching for someone to fill my loneliness. Apollo was often with me but he could not hold me in his arms in the dark of night. I am a woman. A living, breathing soul with the same needs as other people. We humans are social animals, requiring others of our kind, or else we go mad.

In my tent one night during our trek back to Delphi I ruminate about Heraclius. The touch of him. The feel of our bodies together. His handsome face. No, I remind myself. His face is no longer handsome, but disfigured. Perhaps his soul is damaged, too. He belongs to Corinne now, while Tydeus is no longer his son. I forgive him and force myself to forget. I will not slander his life and his choices. I hand him over to the gods for their blessings and tranquility.

I think too of Kriton. I am safe with him, but I had felt safe with two men to no avail. Is safety an illusion of my mind? A woman's fantasy? I intuited Kriton's feelings for me all along the war-strewn path, but ignored them. His affection was difficult to accept, while I was still searching for Heraclius. Seeking a future I did not know had been obliterated by the Fates.

I get up, wrap the old red *chlamys* around me, and leave my tent. The night is drizzly while clouds cover the stars. I go to Kriton's tent and scratch at the flap.

"Selene?" He appears at the entrance, astonished to see me standing outside in the gloom. "What are you doing here?"

"Give me a month, Kriton," I tell him. "Let me remain at Delphi for a month. I will have your answer by then."

"May I hope?" he asks.

"There is always hope," I reply tenderly.

"Then I will talk to your god Apollo. Ask him to intervene for me."

I smile with appreciation. "You are a decent man, Kriton."

"You are not wicked, Selene. You are the most remarkable person I have ever met."

* * *

I stay at Delphi for a month, receiving pilgrims, writing, studying, and living in my cave except during bad weather. Sometimes when I remember the past, my sadness for Heraclius overwhelms me.

Apollo reminds me: "Keep loving Heraclius. Just keep loving him."

"I do love him. It is the only cure for love."

Kriton comes to find me in my cave. He has been impatiently marking time, waiting for me and my answer. "Selene," he announces himself at the cave entrance, to hear the most important answer of all. He is no longer dressed as a *hoplite*, armor and helmet gone, wearing a simple *chiton* and *himation*.

"Yes, Kriton."

"Yes?" He enters and takes my hand, questions in his eyes.

"The answer is yes. Everything has changed." I lead him to the stone couch and we sit on the cushion I fashioned, mended countless times.

He has been holding his breath with apprehension and exhales in relief. "Tell me."

I recount the many events:

"Aegeus died in Athens. He fell sick with winter fever, his lungs congested with fluid, and he suddenly drowned within his own body. I forgive him and ask the gods to care for him in the underworld."

"My mother Xanthippe, too, passed before I returned to Delphi, during the time I was on the road with you. They say she perished of womb fever, excess of black bile in her uterus. She is buried next to Demetria. I forgive her as well. We are all prisoners of our destinies, Kriton."

"I agree."

"Phoibe's daughter Melita married a stone cutter and lives in Athens."

"Aegeus made no provisions for Ianthe of the violet eyes. The unfaithful concubine left with as much coinage and other valuables as she could carry away."

"My son Tydeus is eight years old now. Timon, his guardian, unfortunately despises me. Timon refuses to allow Tydeus to leave Athens, while he administers the huge estate for the boy."

"Even though I was lawfully married to Aegeus, I am not entitled to his wealth nor his property nor his son. I harbor no hard feelings, as those will only hurt myself. After many years of listening to Apollo, I realize there are no bad people. Only ill-fated events that each person must deal with in his or her own way. Anyway, I prefer peace. I want to live simply with a good man."

I finish my protracted litany.

Kriton's kind, rugged face is bathed in smiles hearing my words. "I am a good man," he murmurs to me.

"Yes. A very good man."

"That means…"

"…I am leaving my cave," I finish his sentence. "We may live in the white house together as it is now abandoned. We can marry or not marry. I don't care. No one in the village will mind either. Marriage can enslave women and corrupt men."

"I care, Selene. I would be proud and honored to be your husband."

"I accept, dear one."

Kriton puts his arms around me and hugs me close then we kiss for the first time. I love the feel of him. Manly.

"You are solid. Like the rocks of Delphi."

* * *

Kriton and I move into the white stucco house at the edge of Delphi village to live together as husband and wife, collecting the small bed and other belongings I had left at the cave. He has forsworn his armor, *himation* and helmet, for the life and clothing of an ordinary man.

After we are settled, Kriton cautions me. "I cannot sit around every day, Selene. There must be important work I can do," he says. "I am used to physical labor. Without which I will wither like a tree without water."

"Why don't you talk to the villagers? See if you can be of help with any of their projects, gardens, or building."

"What a wonderful idea, dearest. Could you introduce me to them?"

"Of course."

The next day we stroll hand in hand down the well-worn path to Delphi village, to the house of Kleida. The simplicity of holding his hand feels uplifting. Who could have known that such bliss can be found in the hand of one's cherished husband?

As usual Kleida is outside cooking food. "Are you settled in the white house, Lady Selene?"

"Yes, thank you. I'd like you to meet my husband Kriton. This is Kleida, the most well-known woman in our community."

"After the Delphic Oracle and you of course, Lady Selene." She wipes her hands on her soiled *chiton* and bows. "It is a great honor, Sir."

"Greetings, Kleida. Please call me Kriton."

"What can I do for the two of you today? My daughter will bring your dinner later as customary."

"Kleida, there are no Oracles living in my house, so you do not have continue the responsibility of cooking."

Kriton interrupts us. "Having a vocation is important, so that one has standing in the village and a purpose for living."

"That is true, Sir," Kleida agrees. "I am used to cooking for the women in the white house. Without which I would be worthless."

"You and I are in same predicament, Kleida. I used to be a soldier, but I have no function currently other than being Selene's husband. I have come to see you because I wish to be of service to Delphi village, to help wherever I can."

"There is always so much to do here," she exclaims eagerly. "I will tell my husband and they can discuss projects with you."

"I am gratified, Kleida." He grins. "I have my Thessalian horse and Lady Selene's pony, both of which will come in handy for whatever jobs might be forthcoming. My horse is old, like me, but strong, while the pony is young and hardy."

"Oh, Sir! I cannot express what those animals can do to ease our labors."

Kleida's husband takes Kriton to visit the village men the following morning. Kriton's work in the village brings him happiness while his strong back, numerous skills, and two sturdy animals benefit the village immeasurably. Every night my husband comes home to me tired but in good spirits.

I share my precious scrolls with Kriton, while he becomes as fascinated in them as I have been. We often have philosophical discussions before we retire for the evening. Then we cuddle, sometimes make love, and share our bodies along with our minds. Loneliness is a thing of the past. For both of us.

One night before bed Kriton says to me: "Selene, I wish to read a poem to you that I wrote."

As he begins, he takes hold one of my hands, embracing it to his chest.

"I fell for her
I kissed her
I was lucky.
I am loved.
But who I am,

and who she is
and how it happened
god only knows."

"I am a most fortunate woman," I tell him.

* * *

Bringing morsels of food and other offerings for their spirits and to please the gods, I visit Xanthippe's and Demetria's gravesites regularly. With Xanthippe dead and buried, pilgrims continue to find me and ask for messages. I cannot turn them away. They are starved for answers. I understand their hunger.

Although I'm not yet old, my health is slowly deteriorating, while I now have difficulties with breathing and declining energy. Climbing the strenuous path to the cave has become unfeasible as I need to rest often. My knee pains me, too, which makes walking and hiking ever more demanding. No one appreciates these challenges except Kriton, who lovingly attends me. Perhaps it is due to the difficult time following the birth of my son. Or the long trek to find Heraclius, sleeping outside in cold and wet weather. I don't know.

"My dear wife, I worry about you. Please don't go to the cave anymore, as it taxes your wellbeing with every climb. Why don't you have pilgrims come see you in our little house instead? You will have time and privacy as I am gone most every day."

"Yes, Kriton, you are sensible as usual. I will do as you recommend."

He holds me tenderly. "Years of travel, worry and grief have taken their toll on you. You must let me care for you."

"I am in your capable hands, husband."

I turn down the offer to become the next Pythia. If I became the

Oracle, I would have to relinquish my dear husband, which is un-thinkable.

* * *

Everything changes.

* * *

A new Pythia is installed at Delphi who sits upon Apollo's throne in the *Adyton*. Pilgrims are delighted at her abilities, for which I am pleased. A home is made for her at Kleida's cottage in Delphi village.

* * *

When Tydeus comes of age, my adult son sends for me. I travel to Athens with Kriton, my darling husband, at my side. He rides his vigorous horse while I travel on the *Pindos* pony, as we leisurely trek with a group of pilgrims returning from Delphi.

* * *

"Mother," my son greets me warmly when we arrive at the villa. "We have not seen each other in a long time. Did you have a pleasant trip?"

"Thank you, Tydeus. Our journey was good enough. Are you well?"

"Very well, mother. And how are you?"

"I am tolerable, my son."

"You must be Kriton." Tydeus clasps the man's arm in welcome.

"I am honored to meet the son of Selene," the erstwhile soldier replies, and returns the hearty welcome.

"You will meet my wife Iris when she returns from the Agora. We married just recently, once I reached adulthood. You will like her, mother. She is beautiful and well-educated. Like you."

"I'm sure I will adore her, Tydeus."

"Enough of small talk. Let us be seated in comfort on the patio. I want Kriton to join us as well. There will be no secrets among us. I have good news for you, which cannot wait. Afterwards we will eat and you can rest after your long trip."

When the three of us have seated ourselves on chairs, with cushions of various colors, Tydeus opens a scroll to show me. "I am now the sole owner of my father's estate, properties, ships, and all goods."

"That is wonderful, Tydeus!" I exclaim. "I am happy for you."

"Iris and I will be comfortable," he says with understated humor. "Furthermore, I have granted Timon some of the estate to pay him as my father's executor. He has fallen onto hard times."

"I'm sorry to hear about his misfortune. Your payment is fair and honorable," I tell him.

"Yes. I learned fairness and honor from you," he answers.

His words move me deeply and I blurt out feelings. "I'm sorry that I deserted you, my son. You did not deserve my behavior."

He shrugs with kindness. "All that is in the past, mother. We start anew today. From now on you and Kriton must live here and enjoy Aegeus' wealth with me and my wife. We will get to know one another. I want my family close around me. I have been alone long enough. Loneliness is unbearable."

I am flabbergasted at his generosity. "Yes, I agree."

"There is a price to be paid, though," he grins. "You must continue your work as Apollo's messenger, while you live here in comfort in Athens. It will be a difficult task, I'm sure," and he chuckles.

Where does he get his humor? From Heraclius. Generosity? From Aegeus. He has characteristics from both his fathers.

Then Tydeus becomes solemn and his blue eyes sparkle. "There is no one else like you, mother. Apollo chose you wisely. I want the world to experience the insight and wisdom that comes through you from the god."

"You honor me too highly."

"No. I honor you with good reason."

Kriton speaks, tenderly reaching for my hand, "as do I."

"Promise me, also, that you will teach knowledge as found in the scrolls to my future children. Boys and girls alike," he continues, with emphasis. "I intend to collect a library of scrolls here at the villa, hopefully from around the world. There is much to be learned from great minds."

"You amaze me, especially for one so young. Where do you get your wisdom, Tydeus?"

"From you, mother."

"Feelings are my messages," Apollo tells me.

* * *

Kriton and I live the rest of our days with our family at the exquisite villa in Athens. I present the precious Cycladic statuette to Tydeus to put on display in the *oikos*. I arrange to donate the white stucco house to Delphi Temple, thus creating a permanent home for Oracles.

* * *

Battles between Sparta and Athens and their allies continue sporadically both on sea and land.

* * *

Once Kriton and I are ensconced at the villa, Tydeus joins me as I rest peacefully in the courtyard enjoying bird songs and a cooling breeze.

He sits next to me and gently touches my hand. "Mother. I have an important question for you."

"What do you wish to know, my son?"

"My father," he fumbles. "For years I have known that Aegeus adopted me."

"Yes. That is the truth."

"Thus my father is not Aegeus."

"No…" I equivocate.

"Please tell me all the details. I need to know."

"All right." Clearing my throat, I begin the tale. "Since a child I was in training to become a Delphic Oracle."

"That much I know."

"I did not want to be an Oracle."

"And yet you are a Seer."

"That is different, Tydeus."

"In what way?"

"I do not sit in the *Adyton*, overcome with fumes from the sacred grotto. I hear Apollo clearly without any assistance."

"I see." He leans towards me, to distinctly hear every word.

"Furthermore, all pilgrims are encouraged to ask their questions of the god through me. Not just wealthy or powerful people. Everyone is welcome—including women. Regardless of their status or worldly goods." I am warming to my subject.

"I understand. Where does my father enter into this story? My father is not Kriton, is he?"

"No, dear one. I met Kriton long after you were born."

"Then who is my father?" Tydeus becomes insistent. "I want to know the truth, Mother."

"Your father made me promise to keep the story from you."

"I am old enough to know the facts. I must grasp the unknown history of my being."

"You are a good logician." I gaze fondly at him.

"Please start with his name."

I remember with a reaction that is more emotional than I could have imagined. "His name was Heraclius."

"Heraclius," he repeats softly. "My father's name is Heraclius."

"Was," I correct him.

"Is he dead?"

"I do not know. He was alive when last I saw him."

"Where was that?"

"In a tiny village called Milossa in Thessaly, overlooking the Aegean. He had changed his name to Alex."

"Tell me about him."

"He was a famous athlete and participated in the Olympic and Pythian Games. Later he joined Athenian troops as a *hoplite* to fight the Spartans. He is very tall with dark hair—like you."

"Did I get my blue eyes from you?"

"Yes. Your father's eyes are green. He is extremely muscular and strong. Extraordinarily charming. Handsome like a Greek god, with a cleft in his chin."

"From Aphrodite."

"Yes."

"Did you love him very much?"

"Oh, dear, Tydeus. I cannot continue. Please do not press me to say more. Pain rises within my chest."

"I am sorry, Mother. I have no desire to hurt you."

"I know, darling boy."

"Do I remind you of him?" he presses on.

"A little, in looks primarily, although you are as tenacious as he is. He is an athlete and a warrior. You became a philosopher. A scholar. A merchant with means, integrity, and a desire to help others. A man who believes that women and men are equal. Whereas... I've said too much." I can tell that Tydeus requires the entire story. He will not be able to accept without specifics. "Is it difficult to ask about him?"

"Yes. Very. Nevertheless I have to know."

"You desire to comprehend everything? There are some unpleasant parts."

"Mother, who was it who taught me about truth and honesty? Who told me that can only be at ease when one knows all details."

I take a deep breath and tell my son about his father. Leaving out no important information. When I come to the part of finding Heraclius at Milossa and the heart-rending story of how he got there, both Tydeus and I become silent. I pause for a few minutes.

Heraclius' son fondly squeezes my hand.

In due course I continue. "I loved your father, Tydeus. I still love him. Every day I ask the gods to bless and care for him, wherever he may be, on earth or in the underworld. Heraclius told me the most valuable gift he could offer me was his seed. He was right. Because here you are."

"Thank you for your honesty, Mother."

"I am proud to tell you of your father, Tydeus. I never met my father nor did anyone describe him to me, an unresolvable mystery. However, you deserve the truth, my son."

At that moment Tydeus' wife, Iris, joins us in the courtyard. "Dear husband," she leans over and kisses him gently on the lips in greeting. "Are you enjoying this lovely day?"

"Very much," he responds.

I nod in reply.

"I have wonderful news for both of you," she continues.

"What is that?" Tydeus asks, somewhat puzzled.

"I cease to bleed," she resumes joyfully.

"You mean…"

"I am carrying your child, Tydeus."

He stands and enfolds his wife. "How splendid, my darling Iris! We were just talking about my father."

Her face glows with happiness. "So now you are about to become a father as well." Iris turns to me. "And soon you will be a grandmother."

At that instant Apollo enlightens me with a timely message: "Iris and Tydeus will have four children. Two boys and two girls. All healthy, intelligent, and to be well-educated."

* * *

For the remainder of my time on earth, I continue to pass on the god's messages while I am seated comfortably in the *oikos* at our family's villa. Apollo sends countless warnings that Athenian warships must not travel to Sicily and to beware of Alcibiades. As promised, I teach my grandchildren from the precious scrolls.

On my last day, as I lay dying, attended by loving family and friends, I recite a sweet farewell to my dearest husband Kriton, written by the famous woman poet Praxilla of Sicyon.

"The fairest thing I leave behind is sunlight,
the shining stars and the full moon's face,
and also ripe cucumbers, and apples, and pears."

"Being with you has made me a fortunate man," Kriton tells me as he kisses me goodbye.

* * *

Selene of Delphi, daughter and granddaughter of Delphic Oracles, became the most celebrated Seer in Greece, as well as an eloquent philosopher and poet. Throughout her life Selene spoke of equality for women and wrote treatises against the brutality and insanity of war. She is survived by her beloved husband Kriton, as well as her cherished son Tydeus and his family.

* * *

AFTER NOTES:

The Peloponnesian War began in 431 BC and ended 27 years later. Athenian warships, led by Alcibiades, were destroyed by Sparta at Sicily, as massive death and destruction took place during a confused and disorderly battle.

The Athenian navy forthwith surrendered to the Spartan commander Lysander. Sparta and the Peloponnesian League thus won its greatest victory over Athens and its allies, ending the lengthy Peloponnesian War.

After the war, Athens was overrun by Sparta and other members of the Peloponnesian League, who dismantled the Great Wall around the city, including at the harbor at Piraeus.

After a long and costly war, complicated by plague, Athens never recovered her former power and glory.

Classical Athenian Greece was the initiator and leader of civilization in such diverse subjects as: art; philosophy; poetry; naval warfare; history; technology; mathematics; science; astronomy; playwriting; medicine; geometry; architecture; athletic competition; sea-faring commerce and trade; democracy; debate; and rational thinking.

I acknowledge the following with many thanks:

Song of Wrath: The Peloponnesian War Begins , J.E. Lendon
Soldiers and Ghosts: A History of Battle in Classical Antiquity, J.E. Lendon
The Road to Delphi: The Life and Afterlife of Oracles, Michael Wood
The Oracle:: Ancient Delphi and the Science Behind its Lost Secrets, William J. Broad
Sexual Culture in Ancient Greece, Daniel H. Garrison
The Love Life of the Ancient Greeks , Sofia A. Souli
Delphi , Manolis Andronicos
The Song of Eros: Ancient Greek Love Poems
Sappho, A New Translation, Mary Barnard
The Greek Poets: Homer to the Present, Editors: Peter Constantine; Rachel Hadas; Edmund Keeley; Karen Van Dyck,
Crucible of Civilization documentary, narrated by Liam Neeson

MY GREEK WARRIOR

I loved a man.
Not for a few turns of the sun
Followed by
separation or divorce.
Not for a lifetime.
Growing old
till death do us part.
But for two thousand years.
Waiting.
Hoping.
Praying.
Then having to finish.
Give up.
Relinquish
In anguish
All that he meant to me.
Nuances,
shades,
tones,
touches,
traces,
memories,
hurts,
and raptures.
Continuously
carried
until now.
Craving to resume
but cannot.
Whatever the cost,
whatever the loss,
that lifetime must be torn from this flesh
forever.
Done.
Gone.
The flame extinguished.

For James

Lauren O. Thyme, Aug. 16, 2018

www.ingramcontent.com/pod-product-compliance
Lightning Source LLC
Chambersburg PA
CBHW030250270626
47156CB00021B/1200